I0784017

THE HOLLOWING

STONE EUGENE CLARK

© 2025 Stonefire Press

All rights reserved. No part of this publication may be reproduced, distributed, or transmitted in any form or by any means without the prior written permission of the publisher.

Published by Stonefire Press

Cover art by Shoaib @shoaibpak716

Interior design by Stone Eugene Clark

Printed in the United States of America

DEDICATION

To the lost, the silenced,
and the ones who were never truly forgotten.

EPIGRAPH

I was the girl they buried in silence.
I became the mother who would not forget.
And when the earth refused to speak—
I rose.

I rose in mirrors.
In breath.
In daughters.
In ash.

He thought he could carve me from memory.
But memory is the oldest blade.
And I am its hand.

This is not his story.
It never was.

This is the sound of the hollow breaking open.

—Temperance

AUTHOR'S NOTE

This novel is a work of fiction.

It is inspired by true events and real people, but the characters and scenes are the product of imagination. Names have been changed out of respect for the victims and their families. I have chosen to fictionalize certain timelines, conversations, and details in order to explore the emotional truths of grief, silence, and survival through a narrative lens.

While some elements mirror public cases, The Hollowing is not a documentary. It is a novel about the shadow that violence leaves behind—and the voices that rise from it, demanding to be heard.

This book is, in part, a tribute to those whose stories have gone unheard.

Its chronology may falter because the truth did. The silence came first. The reckoning took half a century.

CONTENTS

CHAPTER 1:
THE FIRST HUNGER

Holland, Michigan – 1971

Some stories are not told in order. They return as the mind remembers them: fractured, out of time, shaped by what could not be spoken when it mattered most.

Beneath the skin of the world, something stirred.

It was not born in the way of men, nor summoned in the manner of devils. It pressed through—a whisper turned scream, a shadow blooming through the softest part of the world.

The vessel, not yet understood as flesh or man, softened in its core. Its chest did not break—it sighed open. A wet tear through layers of skin, sinew, and bone. The cage parted with a soundless breath, and the darkness that had waited inside stepped forward.

It came with no name. No memory. No language. Only the gravity of creation, as if the gods themselves had looked away.

Only hunger.

The air did not shift around it.

The air was it.

The cold wasn't something it passed through—

It was the breath inside its chestless body.

The frost clung to branches like veins, and the branches moved—just barely, just enough—because something beneath them uncoiled.

A knot in the trunk of the nearest tree widened. Not suddenly. Not violently.

Like a yawn.

Like an old wound remembering how to weep.

Bark creaked.

Fibers separated along grain lines no longer straight.

And from the split, a shoulder pushed free—wet and crooked, the color of soaked leaves.

Then ribs. Then a throat.

It did not exit the tree.

It unspooled from it.

As if it had always been part of the wood, sleeping in the xylem, dreaming in the knots.

It hung half-inside the trunk for a moment.

Listening.

Not with ears.

With something older.

Then, with soundless grace, it twisted fully out and onto the forest floor—still moist, still fragrant, like something newly born and already rotting.

This was no man.

Not yet.

This was suggestion.

The idea of a man filtered through hunger and shadow.

The arms hung too long. The knees bent too softly.

Its chest pulsed—just once—as if remembering how lungs once worked.

Then it split.

A gash opened where ribs had fused, and something darker peered from inside.

The air bit with late-winter cold. Gravel shifted beneath something weightless yet tethered. It did not know shoes or the function of breath. But it knew rhythm. It knew gravity. It knew the scent of blood in the wind.

The vessel did not move.

It peeled.

From inside it, the demon—whatever had waited inside the bark-flesh and bone—pressed forward.

The vessel sagged, ribs loosening.

The skin around its chest shimmered and split again. Not with violence, but with urgency.

Like something beneath it had grown too large for its casing.

And from the rupture, it watched her.

Not with eyes.

With intention.

A narrow road curved before it—lined with trees that watched and ditches that swallowed sound. The moon hovered, disinterested. A flicker of streetlight quivered like a warning.

And there—

The girl.

She ran with grace, her form confident, breath visible in small silver puffs. Her body moved in rhythm, as if to music heard only by the bones. Only the cadence of breath and footfall—the heartbeat of her own solitude.

Her name was Maren.

Not spoken aloud—not now—but alive in her lungs as she ran. She always ran when the world felt too heavy to carry. Tonight, it was her mother's silence that chased her, not fear. Her ponytail swung like a metronome. She counted her strides: six per breath, three per heartbeat, two per thought.

She did not know this would be the last night her name belonged only to memory.

She was flushed from motion and chilled by the air, cheeks glowing faintly. The scent of her reached it—not through nostrils, but through the absence.

Something inside the vessel cracked.

Not rage.

Not hunger.

Permission.

The shell split further. The demon slipped forward.

It followed.

Not with feet. With need.

It did not run. It pulled the world toward it—

light bent slightly, silence deepened.

What chased her was not steps behind her.

It was already in the shadows ahead.

A porch light blinked far behind her. Beyond the road, fields yawned—open, black, silent.

She slowed.

Something inside her responded to the quiet. To the wrongness of it. She turned her head.

Saw nothing.

Still, she knew.

The form moved.

It slipped from the ditch with stillness more than motion. A shadow stepping free of a deeper shadow. The form it wore—only vaguely human—twisted in the dark. Its breath did not fog. Its face did not hold expression.

Half-swallowed by the tree, the vessel watched. Still seeing. Still letting it happen.

She ran.

Her scream cracked the night open.

The hunger followed.

Faster than memory. Faster than reason.

The girl turned into a side path, limbs pumping, braid flaring behind her. She darted between fences, passed a parked car, struck the edge of a trash can. Her breath came in bursts. Windows blinked behind her. No one opened a door.

The hunger surged.

The hunger guided the shape with purpose.

The form lunged.

They collided.

She collapsed to the ground, her palms tearing against gravel. She kicked, struck out, connected with something that should have been flesh but gave too much.

Her eyes locked with it.

There was no face. Not truly. Just suggestion—sunken places where eyes might have been. A blur of something once meant to resemble a mouth. And in the chest, a circle—not painted, not worn, but opened—a pit of dark, pulsing absence. A forgotten eye, waiting to remember itself in the world.

The blade grew.

From within. A bone-shard blooming like a fang, curling out from the palm. Obsidian, liquid, silent.

Clothes cut –

flesh pierced.

She screamed again.

The blade whispered through her.

Her body jolted once. Then twice. Then nothing.

The hunger did not howl. It settled.

The form crouched beside her. It tilted its head. Reached a clawed hand and placed something like a kiss against her cheek.

It did not know why.

Perhaps to remember.

But there was still no memory. Only silence.

A sound behind them—a slamming door. A bark. A voice calling a name.

The hunger twisted.

The shape shuddered. The skin recoiled. The blade folded inward, bone sliding beneath muscle. The circle in the chest pulsed once.

The shadow collapsed inward.

The demon stilled.

It stood there—alone on the road.

A shape. Empty. Unnamed.

It turned.

And slithered into the dark – toward the husk it once called home.

Far behind the ribs, the black circle sealed shut.

But something else remained.

A flicker. Not of remorse. Not yet.

Recognition.

As if the hunger itself had glimpsed something other.

Not within her.

Within itself.

The hunger had fed, but in its wake, the silence grew teeth – and it was already gnawing its way back to the surface.

CHAPTER 2

THE MIRROR

Muskegon, Michigan – Early Spring 1971

There was a stillness in the house that felt different tonight.

Miriam couldn't explain it. Not fear. Not sadness.

Something quieter. Like the pause between one thought and the next.

The light in the hallway seemed dimmer than usual, though the bulb had not changed. The air, tinged with lavender polish and a trace of last night's roast, moved softly through the rooms.

And yet something else lingered. Something unnamed.

She moved through the living room with deliberate steps, the soft click of her shoes echoing faintly on the wood floor. The grain beneath her soles felt familiar, worn smooth by years of pacing—her mother's, her father's, her own.

From the kitchen came the sound of running water, dishes being stacked, the low murmur of the radio humming out the evening news. Her mother's voice rose faintly over it—talking to no one in particular, maybe to herself, maybe to the plates.

Outside, the last breath of winter flustered against the glass panes. The sky, drained of color, pressed close to the windows. Shadows pooled in the corners of the room.

Her father sat in his usual chair, worn leather cracked along the arms. Glasses perched low on his nose, he flipped slowly through a tattered issue of *National Geographic*. He cleared his throat from time to time, but otherwise made no sound.

In the far corner, her younger brother James sat cross-legged on the carpet, immersed in a whispered war between his toy soldiers. The little plastic men had seen years of battle; their painted faces faded, some missing limbs. Beside him, Daisy—the family beagle—dozed with one ear lifted, paw twitching in some private dream.

Miriam paused to watch them all.

This was her house, her world. And still, on nights like this, it felt like a stage just waiting for the curtain to rise.

"What time is Harlan coming, honey?" her mother called from the kitchen.

"Seven," Miriam replied, smoothing the front of her blouse. "He said he'd be here right after his chores."

Her mother appeared in the doorway, towel in hand, damp curled ringlets clinging to her temple. "You look lovely. But let the boy talk a bit tonight, hmm? Don't interrogate him like last time."

Miriam gave her a look. "I didn't interrogate. I asked perfectly normal questions."

Her mother smirked. "Normal for a hiring manager, maybe. Not for a girl on her third date."

James snorted. Miriam stuck her tongue out at him, just enough to provoke a giggle.

She excused herself down the hallway toward the mirror mounted beside the front closet.

It had been a wedding gift –

from her grandmother to her mother, a family heirloom belonging to the women of their family. And it would go to her when on her wedding day.

Heavy mahogany.

And at the crown, a carved phoenix, its wings spread, its beak raised toward something unseen.

The glass itself was hand-beveled,

Still clear in the center,

But rippled faintly at the edges.

Miriam adjusted her necklace—a silver chain, simple but meaningful. Her aunt had sent it last Christmas with a note that read: *For the version of you that's coming.*

She leaned closer.

The mirror reflected a girl who looked nearly grown, but not quite.

Her hair—rounded at the edges, curled under with care—framed her face in soft waves. A few rebellious strands had already begun to fall forward. She pushed them back and reached for the Aqua Net, giving two light sprays. The scent was familiar and faintly medicinal.

Her glasses—dark-rimmed cat-eyes—rested snugly on her nose. She'd considered going without them tonight. But they were part of her now. Part of the girl she knew how to be.

Behind the lenses, her eyes looked larger than life.

Wide. Serious. Curious.

Too much of something, not enough of something else.

Her blouse—a powder-blue button-up tucked into a gray skirt—fit just right, modest but feminine. She didn't feel beautiful.

But she looked right.

Neat.

Presentable.

Good.

She hadn't dated many boys. And Harlan… Harlan unsettled her in ways she couldn't name. He was polite. Composed. A little older. He listened. Not the way boys at school did—half-distracted, performative. Harlan heard things.

And sometimes, when he wasn't speaking, he stared—too long, too still—at spaces where nothing was.

A knock at the door.

Miriam's breath caught.

She turned from the mirror, heart suddenly alive in her throat. Her father was already rising. He folded the magazine, set it aside. Daisy gave a single bark and trotted to the door.

He opened it just as Miriam appeared at the end of the hall.

Harlan stood in the frame, shadow behind him, shoulders faintly hunched as if bracing against the cold.

"Evening," he said. His voice was steady, cheerful.

Miriam stepped forward with a shy smile.

He looked fine.

Shirt buttoned, jacket neat enough.

But the details—the ones she noticed without meaning to—were off.

His jacket was buttoned unevenly. A leaf clung to the cuff of his pants. His hair, combed back, was damp at the temples, like he'd walked through mist.

He wasn't quite handsome.

His features were too soft in some places, too hollow in others. The mustache made him look older, more serious than he seemed to be. But his eyes—when they met hers—were unreadable.

Not warm. Not cold.

Just still.

"You okay?" she asked gently.

"Yeah," he replied, brushing a hand through his hair. "Car stalled for a bit. Had to push it off the shoulder. Sorry I'm late."

She nodded. He offered his arm.

"Back by ten," her mother called, drying her hands on the towel.

"Yes, ma'am," Harlan answered, polite as always.

They stepped out into the cold. Daisy whimpered once, then returned to her post beside James.

The car waiting in the driveway was a metallic-blue Oldsmobile

Toronado, its body broad and gleaming faintly under the porch light. The engine idled low, a grumble beneath its polished exterior.

Harlan opened the door for her, and she slid inside. The seat was cold, the interior smelling faintly of cologne and the sweet tang of gasoline.

"You hungry?" he asked as they pulled onto the road. "There's that diner off Broadway. We could get burgers...."

She smiled. "That sounds perfect."

The car moved through the neighborhood, past silent houses and shuttered windows. Streetlights flickered on, one by one. Telephone poles blurred past her window like pacing sentinels.

"What music do you like?" he asked suddenly.

She turned to him. "Simon & Garfunkel. The Supremes. I like voices that sound like they're telling secrets."

He chuckled softly. "That's a good way to put it."

She watched the way he tapped his fingers on the wheel—rhythmic, deliberate. As if keeping time with something only he could hear.

At the diner, they found a booth near the window. A waitress with a faded apron brought them burgers and vanilla shakes. Harlan asked about school, and Miriam told him about her English project. He listened, nodded. Smiled when appropriate.

But sometimes, mid-conversation, his gaze drifted—out toward the parking lot, or to the reflection in the diner glass.

"You sure you're okay tonight?" she asked, stirring her straw.

"Yeah. Just a lot on my mind."

She didn't press. The quiet in him was part of what she liked.

After dinner, they returned to the car. Harlan took a turn she didn't recognize.

"Where are we going?"

"There's a place by the lake. I thought maybe we could sit a while."

She hesitated, then nodded. "Alright."

The road narrowed. Trees pressed close. The world beyond the headlights vanished into black.

He pulled into a gravel turnout, the lake stretched ahead, silver under the moon. The engine cut. Silence settled like snow.

"It's beautiful," she said.

"You are," he replied softly.

She turned, unsure of what to say. He reached out, touched her cheek. Then leaned in.

His lips were dry. Tentative. Not unpleasant—just unfamiliar. His hand moved to her waist, fumbled slightly. The pressure was too firm, not cruel but clumsy.

She pulled back. "Harlan… maybe not so fast."

He blinked. Nodded. "Of course. I'm sorry. I just… I really like you."

"I like you too."

And she did.

He looked away, jaw tight. Fingers flexed once around the steering wheel.

The lake shimmered, still and wide.

She opened her door slightly, let the night air touch her. Somewhere, a loon cried across the water.

He started the car.

"Want to grab a milkshake before I take you home?"

She smiled. "Sure."

The road back felt quieter. He said little.

She didn't mind.

When they pulled into her driveway, the porch light was on. Her father's silhouette lingered in his chair by the window. The house was still.

Harlan walked her to the steps.

"Thanks," she said, pausing.

He nodded. "See you soon?"

She nodded back. "I'd like that."

He waited until she was inside. She waved once through the glass.

In the hallway, the mirror waited.

She stood before it again.

Same girl. Same blouse. Same necklace.

And yet—something had changed.

Her cheeks were flushed. Her bun loosened slightly.

But it was her eyes.

They were different.

Not afraid.

Just… watchful.

She touched her cheek where he had touched it.

Her fingers trembled.

And in the mirror—just for a moment—something shifted.

Like a figure stepping back.

A presence retreating behind her reflection.

She turned.

The hallway was empty.

Daisy let out a low bark from the living room.

Then silence.

The mirror stilled.

And outside, beyond the walls, the wind carried something strange through the trees.

Not a whisper.

But an echo.

Of something that had already begun.

CHAPTER 3

THE SECOND LURCH

Somewhere in West Michigan – 1972

It stirred again.

Not with surprise—not like the first time.

No. This time, the vessel welcomed the fracture.

The skin had grown softer still. The sternum sighed open like parted lips. Muscle folded aside without protest. And from within, it stepped.

There was no fear. No confusion. No birth.

Only continuation.

The hunger had waited nearly a year.

And now, the veil was thin again.

The gravel road before it bent like the neck of a sleeping animal. On either side, fields breathed in slow hushes. Corn stalks stood shoulder to shoulder in silent congregation. Dandelion seeds danced like drifting prayers. The sun had gone, but the night had not yet arrived. This, the in-between, was its hour.

It crossed the threshold of dusk and glided over gravel with feet that left no sound.

The vessel was stronger now. Its limbs no longer twitched with hesitation.

Its chest parted with reverence—like a temple gate, like a ritual wound reopening.

The ribs unfolded. The skin split with grace.

And from within, the demon stepped—fluid, whole, separate.

Not born. Remembered.

The vessel sagged in place, half-curled, half-eaten by shadow and root.

Its eyes did not move.

But it watched.

The demon had become more than shadow.

It had become form.

And ahead—

The girl.

She walked with rhythm. Unbothered. Alone. Her arms swung in soft arcs, her hips shifting with the ease of repetition. Her backpack thumped lightly against her spine. Her ponytail, tied with a fraying ribbon, lifted with every other step. She was humming.

The tune was ordinary.

But the cadence of her breath—ah. That was not.

The demon inhaled the pattern of it, slow and steady. Familiar.

It had heard this music before. Not the melody. The life inside it.

Her blood sang.

And the hunger, having once been fed, remembered the shape of satisfaction. But also the ache that followed.

It moved from the trees.

Not rushed.

Not hidden.

Simply present.

She paused.

Turned.

The hush settled around them.

Nothing moved.

Still, she knew.

She turned again, faster now. Her breath shifted to short, measured bursts. She walked off the road and onto a path that curved between barns, a shortcut etched into the land by generations of passing feet.

The demon followed.

There was no malice in the way it moved. Only purpose.

It stepped across broken stalks. Between fenceposts. Past rusted wire and forgotten pails. It followed her scent—salt and skin and something bright.

And when it reached the corner where the barn wall met the shadows—

She turned again.

And saw it.

The scream that left her throat was jagged—alive.

It inhaled her fear like scent, pulled it into the hollow place behind its ribs. The circle there pulsed once, soft and golden at the edge like blood warmed by breath.

She ran.

Shoes slipping on gravel. Elbows pumping. Her lungs working in bursts.

The demon quickened.

Not sprinting.

Drifting.

It was not a chase.

It was a procession.

She stumbled once—just enough.

The demon caught her before the ground did. It collapsed her into the dry furrow between buildings, her hands catching earth, her cheek striking gravel. She turned beneath it—writhing, clawing, striking with the desperate strength of someone who has not yet accepted what the dark already knows.

Their eyes met.

And in her face, the demon saw it again: recognition.

Not of what it was.

But that it was real.

It hated that.

It pressed her down.

The blade began to bloom.

From the palm—a slow unfurling.

It did not burst forth this time. It emerged. Ritualistically. Lovingly.

Like a petal from a blackened flower, turning outward in wet spirals. Obsidian. Seamless. A sheen of breath clung to its edge, though it had never drawn air. At its base, the flesh of the hand split open in a silent gasp.

The blade pulsed.

The girl struggled harder.

Her hands struck its chest, its jaw, the empty suggestion of where a face should have been. Her cries bent the air.

The demon did not flinch.

It lowered the blade.

The point hovered just below her ribs.

And then—

A single, fluid motion.

No scream this time.

Just breath leaving.

The body arched.

Once.

Then again.

The blade whispered its way through her, not slicing, not stabbing— but entering.

Claiming.

The demon watched her mouth open in a soundless plea. Her fingers spasmed, reaching for something sacred—her throat, her cross, the sky, the stars.

None answered.

The light in her eyes dimmed—not suddenly, but with the slow, reluctant retreat of memory.

The vessel exhaled.

And the hunger settled.

It did not feast.

It did not roar.

It simply… quieted.

The blade retracted slowly, folding back into the palm like a secret sheathed. The skin closed around it like lips after a kiss.

The demon remained above her.

It studied her face.

And in a gesture it did not understand—it leaned down and placed its mouthless face near hers.

No sound.

No language.

Just a pulse. A breath. A moment of breathless silence pressed between their forms like a veil.

Its fingers brushed her cheek.

They left no mark.

But they remembered.

The body stilled.

A thin line of blood had begun to soak the hem of her shirt. It spread, quietly, like a shadow learning how to crawl.

A dog barked in the distance.

A screen door clattered.

The demon rose.

It turned.

And disappeared into the rows of corn.

The earth swallowed its footprints before they cooled.

The breeze, once still, moved again—softly at first. Then with urgency, brushing the girl's hair away from her face.

And far away, someone called her name.

But no one answered.

The demon returned to the clearing—a circle of bent trees and warped grass where light never quite settled.

It knelt.

The hunger was silent now. Not sated, not full.

Just… still.

But something else stirred.

A pulse not born of blood, but memory.

The face.

Her eyes.

The shimmer of knowing that had passed between them.

The demon did not have language for what it felt.

Only this:

The veil had parted again.

And it had passed through.

But this time, something had looked back.

CHAPTER 4:
THE HOUSE ON HACKLEY STREET

Muskegon, Michigan – 1972

The morning began with toast, two cups of coffee, and silence.

Miriam sat at the small, square kitchen table, folding her hands in her lap as the sound of the percolator dwindled behind her. Outside, early spring sunlight dripped through the narrow window over the sink, gilding the counter in quiet gold. She stared at the empty plate in front of her. A single crumb clung to the porcelain.

The house was small, modest, and clean. A starter home, they called it. Years later no one would remember when the shadows began – only that they were already there, watching, even in rooms that felt safe. A place to begin. The wallpaper in the kitchen was pale green, vines climbing in endless, symmetrical trails. She had chosen it herself.

The smell of coffee filled the room—bitter and grounding.

Harlan had already left for work. He had kissed her cheek before walking out the door, his hands rough, his hair still damp from the shower. He had been distracted lately—not cold, exactly, but elsewhere, as though his thoughts had drifted down a corridor she could not follow.

She had told herself it was nothing. That new husbands adjusted in their own ways.

She stood and poured herself a second cup.

The cup was part of a mismatched set, a wedding gift from her aunt. The handle was chipped, but she always used this one. It fit her fingers like it had been made for them.

She sat again. The chair creaked beneath her.

Across the kitchen, their wedding photograph hung on the far wall. She was in her mother's borrowed dress, a simple satin gown with long sleeves and a row of tiny buttons down the back. Her hair had been curled and tucked beneath a white veil. Harlan wore a navy-blue suit. He smiled for the picture.

But in the frame, he did not quite look at the camera.

Miriam frowned and looked away.

A lawnmower started in the distance, the sound blending with the rustling of leaves and the soft murmur of birds. The world outside was shedding winter's hush, but spring in Muskegon never came in all at once. It arrived carefully, like someone knocking at a door they were not sure they should open.

She moved to the sink, rinsed her cup with deliberate care, and set it on the rack to dry.

She wasn't due at the store until noon. Her part-time job at the fabric counter didn't pay much, but it let her be near color and texture. She loved the sound of scissors gliding through cloth, the heft of spools in her hands. There was a rightness in choosing patterns, in watching women search for something simple they could shape with their own fingers—as if stitches might secure what words could not.

Before work, she decided to walk to the market. It wasn't far—just three blocks to a modest storefront. On the way, she passed her neighbor, Mrs. Danvers, crouched in her garden, hands sunk into the earth.

"Morning, Miriam," she called.

"Good morning. They're coming in early this year."

"The earth's waking up," the old woman said. "She always knows before we do."

Miriam smiled, but the words stayed with her.

At the grocer's, the smell of oranges and old wood filled the air. She picked up a dozen eggs, a tin of coffee, a carton of milk. She lingered at the baking aisle, her fingers tracing the tops of flour sacks.

She thought about making pie that weekend. Harlan liked apple. She did too.

Back home, she unpacked the groceries slowly, setting each item in its place, wiping down the counters until the kitchen smelled of soap and something older—something harder to name.

She showered without hurry, letting the steam rise and bead along the mirror. Her reflection blurred, then cleared. She stood there for a long moment, hair hanging damp along her shoulders, the mist lifting around her like a second skin.

She pulled her hair into a loose braid, then dressed in a skirt and pressed blouse. She added a cardigan, though the air was warming.

At her vanity, she dusted powder across her cheeks. Her glasses lay folded beside the mirror. She reached for them, paused.

Her face without them looked softer. Younger. A face that asked to be trusted.

She slid the glasses on.

The house creaked. A familiar sigh in the hallway.

She turned, half-expecting to see—nothing. Only the natural breath of wood and wind.

And yet—

There were moments when the house felt like it was holding something just behind the walls. Not a presence. Not a person. Only the hush before a name is spoken. A weight without sound.

She shook the thought away.

In the bedroom, the bed was still unmade. She crossed to it, smoothing the quilt, tucking the corners precisely as her mother had taught her. On the nightstand, Harlan had left his watch. She picked it up, turned it in her fingers.

The glass was scratched. The band worn thin where it had once been tightened and loosened too many times.

She set it down gently.

At work, the store was slow. Miriam moved among bolts of fabric stacked like spines on a shelf—corduroy, tulle, muslin. A young girl came in with her mother, searching for a dress pattern she had seen on a neighbor.

"I want something like this, but prettier," the girl said, holding out a magazine clipping.

Miriam knelt beside her.

"This one has the same lines," she said, pointing to a simple pattern. "You could use a brighter thread. Scallop the collar. Make it your own."

The girl beamed. Her mother nodded.

After they left, Miriam sat behind the counter, watching dust float in the amber light. For a time, she allowed herself to drift—not asleep, not fully awake either. Somewhere quieter than either place.

She imagined another life. A child at home. A kitchen wide enough for dancing. Harlan laughing at the table. A house filled with books, with music humming through the walls like a second heartbeat.

A different kind of quiet.

Not this hollow one.

Her break ended. She rose, straightened her cardigan, and returned to her place.

That evening, she walked home beneath a lavender sky. The trees blurred their edges against the setting light. The air held warmth, but also memory.

Inside, Harlan was not yet home. She made dinner anyway. Fried chicken. Buttered peas. Mashed potatoes. She lit a candle at the center of the table without thinking about it, though it was not a special occasion.

It simply felt right.

When he came in, he looked tired. Smiled. Kissed her cheek.

"Smells good," he said.

"How was work?"

He shrugged. "Long."

They ate quietly. Miriam filled the spaces between forkfuls with stories from the shop. He nodded at the right times. Asked a question or two. But his eyes never quite settled on her.

After dinner, she washed the dishes while he read in the living room. The pages of his magazine turned in soft, irregular beats. From time to time, he cleared his throat.

She dried her hands. Walked down the hallway toward their bedroom.

Passed the mirror.

Paused.

It had once hung in her mother's house, and her grandmother's before that – a heavy thing of mahogany and gold, its broad frame carved in fretwork so fine it seemed spun from smoke. At the crown, a phoenix spread its gilded wings, its beak tilted skyward as if caught mid-cry. The mirror had been made, her mother said, when America was still a wilderness and England ruled the seas. A wedding gift, passed through the women of her family for generations, it had come to Miriam on her wedding day – wrapped in muslin and memory.

The glass, hand-beveled and still mostly clear, rippled faintly at the edges, softening reflections as if uncertain whether to reveal or conceal.

There was nothing there.

No shadow. No flicker.

Only her reflection, slightly distorted by the age of the glass.

She tilted her head.

Her eyes looked different tonight.

Not afraid.

But waiting. Or wanting.

For what, she could not say.

She turned away. Went to bed.

The house settled around her like a body folding itself inward. A breath held too long.

And the mirror, though still, remembered what it had seen.

CHAPTER 5:
THE ADOPTION

New Orleans – June 1974

"To name a thing is to claim it.
To surrender without naming it is to vanish twice."
— Anonymous,

She was sixteen, and the heat made the world feel fevered.

In the rust-worn halls of Charity Hospital, where the ceiling tiles wept and the walls held secrets behind their chipped enamel, Kathy lay rolled on her side beneath the humming fluorescent light. It did not flicker -- it hummed, low and alive, like something waiting to swallow her whole. The cot beneath her creaked when she moved. The cotton sheet clung to her legs, reluctant to let her go.

She had been in labor for hours, but time had lost its sharpness. There was only the dull roar of her body tearing open, and the pale voices of nurses drifting in and out of earshot, too busy to speak directly to her.

No mother held her hand. No priest came. She thought of asking for one—and then did not. She was not here to be saved. She was here to surrender.

26

They had told her: do not name the child. Not even in thought. To name was to bind. To bind was to bleed.

But Kathy had whispered it for months now, tucked beneath her breath where no hand could reach.

Elara.

The name made her feel weightless, even now, even through the fire inside her hips and spine. It floated her above the steel rails and peeling floors.

Outside, the air smelled of rain on hot concrete. Storm clouds gathered, curling thick and low like beasts behind a curtain.

Something else gathered, too.

Something in the room with her.

It had no shape. No breath. But it waited.

Another contraction ripped through her. She cried out, and for a moment, the walls themselves seemed to pull away.

They brought her to the delivery room. The stirrups were cold. Her gown stained. Someone said to push.

She did.

She pushed as if love itself had become flame clawing out of her. As if birth was not a blessing, but a final act of war.

And when she thought she would tear in two, the world filled with the sharpest, most impossible sound—a child's cry, thin and fierce, cutting straight through the bone of her.

Kathy strained to see.

A glimpse:

— dark hair

— fists wrapped too tight for this world

— the bright, angry flush of a soul not yet resigned.

"Is she alright?" Kathy gasped.

No one answered.

The child was bundled quickly. The movement was practiced, sterile. She saw only a fragment of her—the curve of an ear, the glint of damp skin—and then she was carried away.

"Wait—please—"

But the nurse was already at the door, carrying Elara not cruelly, but impersonally, like a package destined for another life.

As though Kathy had been only the envelope.

The hollow opened inside her then. Not a wound—wounds could heal. A hollow. A space where ribs and skin collapsed inward.

She turned her face to the ceiling and whispered the name once more aloud, fierce against the still air.

Elara.

Something heard her.

Not the nurse.

Not the doctor.

Something above the fluorescent hum, behind the light, in the place grief is given breath.

It was not a demon. Not yet.

But it lingered.

Waiting.

And as Kathy fell into a half-sleep, her arms empty, her body shivering from the sudden loss, something without a name pressed its breath against hers.

She had given birth.

Not all of her had survived.

"What is borrowed by the state is never truly given back."
— Notes from a closed case file

The days that followed bled together, thick and slow.

She remembered the sound of milk boiling over on the stove.

The stained linoleum catching the afternoon light.

The way a baby's breath, warm against her collarbone, could silence every cruel thought the world had ever taught her.

Nine months. Not of possession.

Of presence.

Elara had been hers only in the spaces between paperwork. In the hush between welfare visits. The state would never say she was hers. Not truly.

But Kathy knew the map of her daughter's body:

— the spiral of hair at her crown

— the small arch of her left foot

— the milk-sweet scent of her scalp, a breath softer than prayer.

There were nights when Elara woke crying—not wailing, but the dry, broken whimper of a soul already taught not to expect rescue. Kathy would lift her from the borrowed crib, cradle her tight, whisper songs she made up on the spot, cobbled together from memory and defiance.

Songs her own mother had never sung to her.

Songs stitched with promises.

I will never let the world take you.

But the world is always hungry.

There were nights Kathy felt it—circling. Watching.

Not malice.

Not exactly.

Something older than cruelty. Something that had seen this all before.

Once, she saw it.

Or thought she did.

A shimmer above the crib, a distortion like heat rising from blacktop. No form. No mouth. Just pressure, silent and certain.

Elara had stared into it, unafraid.

Kathy said nothing to her parents.

What use were warnings in a house that had already been breached?

She held her daughter tighter. Whispered the promises again, fierce and failing.

But the papers had been filed.

The caseworker smiled too kindly.

The pastor said God had a plan.

The social worker praised the Rockweillers—stable, educated, ready.

Liars.

She pressed her lips to Elara's soft ear.

"I will not forget you," she whispered.

Nine months passed.

A second labor.

No blood this time.

Only silence.

New Orleans – Spring 1975
"The soul has exits it does not confess."
— Marginalia, unsigned

By spring, the paperwork moved faster than the hours.

She thought signing the papers would be a snap—a final wound—but it was not.

It was slow.

A bleeding from the root.

Her hand moved steadily, mechanically, printing her name neatly on the line.

No one saw the tremor that split her spine beneath her blouse.

No one heard the tear that opened inside her lungs with every breath.

They told her she was brave.

They measured her worth by the cleanliness of her surrender.

As if her soul was a garden to be weeded and approved.

But Kathy had not planted a garden.

She had birthed a star.

And now they buried it beneath forms and signatures and sanctioned forgetting.

That night, she walked the length of Magazine Street under trembling streetlamps.

The city spoke around her—a saxophone crying from a high window, a trolley grumbling its way toward Canal, the laughter of strangers.

It all slid past her like smoke.

She was not fully in her body anymore.

Her hands were cold.

Her breath tasted metallic.

Somewhere deep inside, a door had swung open into a space where time did not pass.

She had signed her name.

And something had broken loose inside her.

It was not grief, not yet. Grief requires recognition.

This was something deeper.

A tearing that no doctor could name.

Her body had stitched itself around Elara for nine months—and now the stitch had ripped upward, through rib and throat and name.

No scar would form.

Only the absence.

Only the howl.

And something in that howl refused to vanish.

The part of her that had held Elara—in womb, in arms, in dream—unlatched itself.

It rose.

Not a ghost.

Not a spirit.

A tether.

It did not linger.

It found the girl.

Not by trail or scent, but by need.

Into the car.

Into the crib.

Into the silence.

Temperance had no voice yet.

Only direction.

She did not hover.

She did not rage.

She moved the way grief moves when it is refused a body to cling to.

Glass windows shimmered along the street.

The air thickened with the scent of jasmine until it clogged her throat like grief made perfume.

Kathy stopped before a church.

The doors were locked.

There was no sanctuary left.

But something watched from the rooftop.

Something perched in the crooked angles of the steeple.

It was not heaven.

It was not hell.

It was what remained.

Kathy stood on the sidewalk, trembling, human still.

But behind her heartbeat, something else lived now.

It had no face yet, no voice.

Only a name whispered into breathless dark:

Temperance.

She would not rest.

Because part of her had already followed the child into the dark.

West Michigan – March 1976
"What is given in silence is taken by shadow."
— Folk saying, West Michigan

The house was too quiet.

Miriam stood at the kitchen window with one hand resting on the sill, the other gently lifting the edge of the curtain. Her gaze drifted over the driveway as though it might bloom with movement if she only waited long enough. The maple tree near the front porch trembled in the wind, its bare branches scratching faintly at the siding—a sound she had long ago learned to ignore but which now seemed louder, more insistent.

She had scrubbed the floor twice already that morning. Once with lemon-scented cleaner, and again with vinegar, to be sure. The scent of it still lingered in the air like something sacred. The baseboards were polished, the windows wiped, the couch cushions beaten and rearranged. Everything must look perfect.

And yet, there was a stillness in the house that refused to be dusted away.

Miriam moved slowly from window to hallway to nursery, checking the room one last time. The pale pink blanket had been smoothed over the mattress, its folded edge exactly parallel with the crib's rail. A stuffed lamb with glass eyes and slightly frayed ears sat propped in the corner. She had ironed the curtains and laid out a storybook on the dresser.

It was not a grand nursery. The wallpaper had faded in one corner where sunlight touched it too often, and the floor creaked when she stepped too near the radiator. But it was clean, and it was quiet, and it was waiting.

She whispered the name aloud as though to test it on her tongue: "Lauren."

A new baby - 9 months old. Quiet. Brown hair, light eyes.

Behind her, Harlan sat at the kitchen table, his spoon clinking rhythmically against the inside of his coffee cup. Stirring and stirring, though the sugar had long since dissolved. He hadn't said a word in ten minutes.

"They said ten o'clock," Miriam said, her voice barely more than breath.

"Still early," he murmured. "People run behind."

She nodded, though her grip tightened on the curtain.

It wasn't supposed to be this cold in March.

Then—the sound. A car door closing.

She froze.

Miriam moved to the door, smoothing the front of her skirt, then brushing invisible lint from her blouse. Her heart beat fast, not with fear, but with something more fragile: hope pressed too tightly beneath her ribs.

When she opened the door, the wind rushed in around her, smelling of dry leaves and faraway fires. On the porch stood a woman in a gray wool coat, tall and sharp-angled, holding a clipboard with the stiffness of practiced formality. Her name tag read: Marla Keene, Child Welfare Services.

In her arms, a baby girl.

She was smaller than Miriam had imagined—delicate, narrow-shouldered, with a secondhand coat buttoned too tightly around her middle. Her shoes, oversized and scuffed, bore the marks of other children. Her hair had not been brushed that morning; it clung to her forehead in damp strands. Her eyes—pale, uncertain—drifted not to Miriam, but past her, into the dim corridors of the house.

"Mrs. Rockweiller?" the woman asked.

Miriam nodded. "Yes. Please—come in."

Marla offered a tight smile. "This is Elara". Elara did not move.

Miriam's lips pressed together. She reached for the child, eyes steady. "Her name is Lauren now."

Her tone was soft, but final – like a door gently closing.

Harlan appeared in the hallway. He didn't speak, but grimaced slightly and offered a smile that didn't quite reach his eyes. "Hi there".

Lauren remained still.

Marla passed the child over to Miriam. Miriam held Lauren carefully, keeping her movements slow. "We're so happy to meet you, sweetheart. You must be tired from the drive."

Nothing.

The girl's eyes wandered the ceiling, the light fixture, the far wall—anywhere but the people.

Then something shifted.

Not in the girl. Not in the room.

Behind them.

The temperature seemed to drop, subtly but noticeably, as though someone had opened a window they shouldn't have. A faint shiver ran through Miriam, and she glanced toward the hallway, seeing nothing.

Unseen, a presence moved.

It passed through the doorframe like mist pulled by memory. It was not a person—not exactly—but a silhouette of memory made real. Its form was feminine, but only barely—hair that wasn't hair drifting in a weightless curl behind it. No face. No hands. Only an impression of sorrow suspended in air.

It did not touch the girl.

But it leaned toward her, as if recognizing something in the shape of her.

Lauren blinked.

"Why don't we show you your room?" Miriam asked, her voice carrying more trembling than she intended.

The caseworker nodded, scribbling something on her clipboard. "I'll follow in just a moment."

Miriam carried Lauren down the hall, Harlan lingering in the kitchen.

The entity lingered behind them all.

The nursery glowed faintly in the afternoon light. Miriam had left the curtains half-drawn to soften the shadows. She gestured toward the crib, "We kept some toys in here. The lamb was mine, when I was little. His name is Thimble."

Lauren did not respond.

Miriam, holding the child, reached slowly toward her hair, brushing it aside gently with her fingers. She found a knot and worked at it carefully.

"I used to have hair just like yours," she said. "Tangles and all."

Lauren turned her head slightly—not away, but not toward her either. Her gaze had fixed on the wallpaper near the ceiling, where the pattern of stars had begun to peel at the edges.

Behind them, the entity hovered. Not menacing. Not warm. Watching.

Miriam reached for the book on the dresser. "Would you like a story before bed tonight? I can read you one. Or we can make up our own."

Lauren did not respond.

The radiator ticked once.

That night, after Marla had departed, after dinner had been eaten in near silence, Miriam lay in bed beside Harlan, whose breathing was even and low.

The moonlight touched the edge of the bedroom curtains.

Miriam turned to face the ceiling.

Something moved in the hallway—so softly that it might have been the floorboards settling. But the sound carried with it a presence. She closed her eyes, listening harder, then shook her head.

"It's just nerves," she whispered.

She pulled the blanket up to her chin and whispered a prayer—not out loud, but in the language of mothers before her: Let her be safe. Let her be whole. Let her love me someday.

Down the hall, something listened.

Not God.

But memory, shaped like a woman who would not go.

Waiting. Watching. Bound by something that refused to let go.

CHAPTER 6:
SPLIT

Grand Haven Township, Michigan – Summer 1980

The skin splits with less resistance now.

It does not burn as before. It welcomes the tear. The vessel has grown softer. More willing.

A seam, not a wound. An invitation, not a rupture.

And the demon is no longer blind.

It knows the cool bite of summer air. It knows the scent of old leaves and oil and damp rubber and sweat.

It knows how blood smells in motion.

It knows this road.

No—not this one. But one like it. The gravel sings the same song beneath its feet.

The girl glides, same as before. Faster this time. Stronger.

She hums.

The vessel crouched low in the ditch—silent, bent, waiting.

And from within, the demon stirred.

It felt something unfamiliar: anticipation.

The ribs opened with quiet certainty.

And the demon stepped forward—wet-jointed and wide-eyed, as if remembering what it had once been allowed to do.

And she sees it.

And the world changes.

Her face twists in that ancient shape—the mask of prey. Her mouth opens but no sound comes, not yet.

Her feet move.

She runs.

The demon moves. A lurch. A stumble.

Then the sound—

Crack.

A branch beneath the vessel's foot.

A betrayal of silence.

The demon's skeletal hand raises. And for the first time, it does not summon the blade.

Something else answers.

From the space just behind its palm, a filament of red light erupts—plasma, searing and sharp.

It tears through the humid air with a hiss like screaming metal, striking the edge of the tree line.

The light is not light.

It bends.

It sings.

It burns without smoke.

The girl screams—at the sound, at the heat, at the thing that should not exist.

And she runs.

But she doesn't fall.

She doesn't trip.

She does not belong to panic.

Her limbs obey her.

The moment is fractured now. The hunger snaps its teeth but finds only distance.

The scent of her fills the air—sweet and iron-wrapped.

But the ground offers no blood.

And then—headlights.

A truck rounds the bend.

Brakes squeal.

A man's voice.

A dog barking.

A door slams.

There are eyes now. Too many.

The demon growls from the inside—not yet, not yet.

But the chest tightens.

The vessel panics.

It has never been seen like this. Not fully. Not exposed.

The girl turns sharply into the grass and disappears into the trees behind the houses.

The man's voice grows louder.

"Hey! Are you alright? I saw something—what the hell—"

Too much light. Too many sounds.

And so it disappears.

* * *

The vessel remained at the edge of the trees—slumped, still watching.

And somewhere deeper, the hunger coiled—tasting failure.

Inside the vessel, the demon thrashes.

It claws at the walls.

It was not ready to retreat.

It was not finished.

This has never happened before. Not like this.

The girl lives.

And that is new.

That is unbearable.

It coils itself within the ribs of the vessel. The plasma—the red stream—still echoes through the limbs, humming in the marrow like a memory trying to become muscle.

It was beautiful.

It was powerful.

And it was useless.

The hunger folds back in.

The skin closes.

But the rage remains.

* * *

It returns to the place between places—a clearing deep in the woods, where roots grow in spirals and even the birds avoid the branches.

Here, the vessel kneels.

The wind does not move here.

The world holds its breath.

The demon stares down at its own hands.

They are hands. They are not hands.

The left still bears the echo of the plasma—fingers seared black along the tips, as though burned from the inside out.

They do not bleed. But they hum.

It flexes them. Slowly.

The face of the girl returns.

She had seen it.

Truly seen it.

There was no veil. No flicker of illusion. No cloak of shadow.

She had turned, locked eyes with the vessel's—

—and did not collapse.

Her scream had been real. But her spine had held.

This is worse than failure.

40

This is humiliation.

The hunger does not understand shame. But the thing within does.

Something deeper than hunger.

Older than flesh.

A name? A wound?

It cannot recall.

But it remembers this:

The mask of prey broke.

And something stared back.

It howls. Not aloud. But in a voice that tears only within.

The air trembles around it.

The soil ripples.

Leaves blacken at the edges, curling like ash.

And the plasma crackles once more beneath the skin of its left arm, eager to be called again.

But it does not call it.

It is thinking.

A sound.

Far off.

The girl. Still running.

Her voice joins another—human, masculine. A man with a flashlight. A leash. A gun, maybe.

They talk about what they saw.

"It looked like a man—no, not a man—Jesus, it lit up—"

The demon listens.

And it learns.

They saw too much.

Not just the girl.

The man. The dog.

The world.

The vessel wraps tighter, clawing at its own ribs from the inside.

It was supposed to be quick.

One pulse. One tear.
Then silence.

* * *

But it missed.
And now it is known.
The rage turns cold.
The plasma retreats.
The hunger sulks in the hollows.
And something begins to harden in the cavity where the black circle pulses behind the sternum.
Not bone. Not blade.
Resolve.
The next time, it will not hesitate.
The next time, there will be no scream.
No truck.
No man.
Only silence.
Only the sound of blood soaking earth.
The demon will wait.
Not long.
Just enough.
Until the girl is alone again.
Or another.
It does not care.
The shape does not matter.
Only the ending.
The rage has quieted.
The hunger has grown teeth.
The vessel is awake now, even when sleeping.
And the world will not look back again.
Because next time, there will be no one left to look.

CHAPTER 7

THE GOODBYE

Muskegon, Michigan – Early September 1980

Miriam folded his shirts with mechanical precision.

One after the other.

Long sleeves first, then the collar tucked neatly inward, the hem creased against the edge of the bed.

Her hands moved without thinking, just as they had the last time he left. And the time before that.

But today, the cotton felt heavier.

As though the fabric held a different kind of memory.

Harlan stood by the dresser, quietly packing his shaving kit into a small duffel. The same duffel he'd used on their honeymoon, worn now along the seams.

She had stitched the fraying handle last spring, but the thread was loosening again.

The room was filled with the rustle of fabric, the quiet click of the closet door, the faint clink of the razor as it slid into place.

Outside the bedroom, Lauren's footsteps padded across the hallway, her voice rising into a quiet song—something about a pony, maybe a song from church.

It was hard to tell.

She always sang to herself when no one was listening.

"How long will you be gone again?" Miriam asked, smoothing the final shirt before setting it beside the bag.

"Just a couple weeks. Maybe less. Navy paperwork. Something about old files they need me to sign."

She nodded once. "Virginia still?"

"Norfolk."

He didn't look at her when he said it.

Miriam picked up the last folded shirt and placed it into the duffel. She zipped it slowly, the sound too loud in the stillness of the room.

She could feel the moment approaching—not an argument, not quite. But something tender on the edge of rupture.

In the kitchen, the coffee pot clicked off with a hollow pop.

She moved to pour a travel cup.

Two spoons of sugar. No cream. Stirred slowly.

She handed it to him without a word.

He took it without meeting her eyes.

Lauren wandered in, cradling her doll by one arm.

She paused when she saw Harlan. "Are you goin' get me a seashell again?"

He crouched beside her, smiling. "You want one?"

She nodded seriously.

"Okay then. Something pink."

"I like the kind that makes the ocean sound," she whispered, clutching the doll tighter.

Harlan placed a hand gently on her head. "I'll find one."

Miriam watched him.

Something in his tenderness felt off—not false, not rehearsed. But too perfect.

Like someone playing the part of a father in a scene he didn't write.

The light in the kitchen shifted. Clouds passed. Shadows returned.

She stepped to the front door, her hand brushing the curtain aside to glance out at the street. The air was warmer than it had been last week. September still carried traces of summer.

Harlan pulled on his coat, slowly. The motion looked stiff, like he wasn't sure which arm to use first.

He looked at her finally. "I should be back by the fifteenth."

"Be careful," she said. The words caught in her throat.

He nodded.

There was a pause.

She wanted to say something—ask if he needed money, ask if this time he might call from the hotel, or ask why he hadn't touched her in two weeks. But the words hung between them like damp laundry.

Heavy. Clinging.

He leaned in and kissed her on the cheek.

His lips were dry.

Then he turned to Lauren and waved. "You be good for Mom, okay?"

She nodded solemnly, eyes wide.

The screen door opened.

Then closed.

Miriam stood at the window and watched him walk down the driveway.

He carried the duffel low on one side, shoulders hunched forward.

His stride was uneven. He did not look back.

Lauren tugged gently at her sleeve. "Will he bring me the shell?"

Miriam forced a smile. "Of course he will."

But something in her chest tightened.

Not dread.

Something quieter.

Like a hand brushing the back of her neck.

Or the moment just before a glass falls.

The car turned the corner and disappeared.

The house was silent.

Later that afternoon, she changed the bedsheets.

Not because they were dirty, but because the room had gone still, and she didn't want the stillness to settle too deep into the linens.

She washed the mugs, re-swept the kitchen floor, and wiped down the top of the refrigerator—someplace no one would see but where dust liked to hide.

Lauren napped on the living room couch, one arm curled around her doll's head. Her lips parted slightly as she breathed, eyes fluttering beneath lids.

The house was too quiet.

Miriam stood at the hallway mirror – the same one her mother had sworn still held dreams.

She adjusted the collar of her blouse.

She wasn't going anywhere. But the act of grooming made her feel present.

Behind her, the corridor yawned.

No sound.

No breeze.

She looked at herself a moment too long.

And then it happened.

A shimmer.

Not a movement. Not a shape.

Just a ripple in the reflection.

Like heat rising from pavement, but vertical, just behind her left shoulder.

She turned.

No one.

The hallway remained empty.

But the light in the mirror flickered—not visibly, not enough to call it dimming—but she felt it.

Like the space between things had shifted.

She looked back into the glass.

Nothing.

But something in her scalp tingled. The back of her neck went cool.

She pressed her lips together and turned away.

"It's just nerves," she whispered.

She went to check on Lauren.

The girl hadn't moved.

That evening, dinner was quiet.

Lauren ate in small bites. Miriam made spaghetti, the simplest comfort she knew.

Neither of them spoke much.

After dishes, Miriam tucked Lauren into bed, brushing her hair with slow strokes.

The girl didn't ask for a story.

She only said, "Tell Thimble not to be scared."

Miriam looked down at the lamb. "Why would Thimble be scared?"

"I think something's watching," Lauren whispered, eyes drifting toward the ceiling. "Not mean. Just waiting."

Miriam froze for half a breath.

Then leaned forward and kissed her on the forehead. "Thimble is very brave."

She turned off the light.

Later, in the bedroom, Miriam lay on her back beside the indentation where Harlan had slept the night before.

The sheets were still warm from the dryer. But the space beside her felt cold.

Not lonely.

Vacant.

The moonlight traced a pale line across the wall.

She closed her eyes, listening.

The wind passed outside the window, pushing gently at the tree branches.

The house settled.

The radiator clicked once.

And then—

Footsteps.

Not heavy.

Just the sound of something crossing the hall. Once. Then gone.

Miriam opened her eyes.

Listened harder.

Nothing.

She didn't move.

Didn't rise to check.

Some part of her had already decided that knowing wouldn't help.

Instead, she pulled the blanket higher and whispered a prayer—

not to God,

but to whatever mother might be listening in the dark.

Let her be safe. Let her be whole. Let her love me someday.

down the hallway, the mirror stood quiet – its mahogany frame dark as dried blood, the phoenix at its crown forever mid-cry, gilded wings outstretched.

No reflection shimmered.

No breath fogged the glass.

But something lingered.

Not Temperance. Not yet.

But the outline of grief, shaped like a woman,

waiting

just beyond the silver.

It did not move.

But it saw her.

And it would not forget.

CHAPTER 8:
BLOOM

The vessel breathes.

Not with lungs. With longing. It draws the humid night into its ribs like a psalm, like the intake of a priest before the bell tolls. And from within the softened layers of flesh, the demon unfolds.

There is no rupture anymore. No tearing. The boundaries have worn thin. The skin opens with ease, as if it remembers now that it was always meant to do so. A curtain pulled aside. A veil dissolved.

And the dark steps through.

And the vessel is no longer needed.

A husk, sloughed like old skin.

A chrysalis, emptied.

What once was borrowed is now born.

Outside, the air clings to the world like wet silk. Jasmine presses against the senses. Somewhere, not far, a train moans its lonely song. But here, beneath the pulse of this Southern night, there is only the hum of the streetlamp and the cool hush of grass beneath feet that do not quite touch the ground.

The house waits ahead. White. Quiet. Modest.

It does not know it is prey.

The demon approaches with calm. The hunger has matured. What once surged now simmers. This is not frenzy. This is sacrament.

It does not knock.

The door clicks open with the soft confidence of memory. It does not creak. It does not resist. Something inside has already said yes.

The entry smells of old wood and wine. Two glasses rest on a side table. One smudged with lipstick. The other still half full. The memory of laughter clings to the cushions. A friend had just left. But the presence lingers. A warmth not yet cooled. The house still breathes her.

The demon inhales.

It pauses in the hallway.

Not from hesitation. From habit.

This is not frenzy. This is preparation.

It turns toward the small alcove where the telephone rests—ivory plastic, coiled cord, waiting like a lifeline. A relic of hope.

The demon lifts the receiver.

It does not speak. It listens.

Not to the dial tone, but to the possibility. The potential of interruption. Of escape.

Then it flexes a stalk of flesh – wet-jointed and pulsing – toward the mouthpiece, with a precision that mimics tenderness, each movement a violation of anatomy.

A twist. A click. The soft shudder of something disassembled.

The cap comes away with ease. Inside, the transmitter rests like a seed.

The demon removes it.

Not torn. Not broken.

Just gone.

It sets the receiver back in its cradle. The phone looks unchanged. Ready. Willing.

But should she reach for it—

No one will hear her.

It is a small thing. A quiet cruelty.

A rehearsal of silence.

Then the demon turns.

It moves soundlessly down the hallway, guided by heat and heartbeat. It does not see in the way of men. It sees veins like rubies and breath like fog in winter. And there—at the end of the hall, behind the cracked door—Celeste.

She is asleep.

One leg drawn up under the sheets. One arm curled near her face. A nightshirt loose over her frame. Her mouth slightly open. A line of light from the window slants across her shoulder.

The room is clean. Ordered. There is care in the way her robe hangs from the door. A candle sits unlit on the dresser. On the nightstand: a paperback novel, a rosary, and a ring removed for rest.

The demon steps through the doorframe.

And she stirs.

Not from noise. From presence.

Her eyes open slowly. Confused. Then aware.

They meet its gaze.

And something inside her breaks.

Not her spine. Not her voice. Not yet.

Her soul flinches.

She moves. Swift. Determined. A sharp inhale and a reach for the lamp. But the demon is already there. It blurs across the space, weightless, sudden. The door closes behind it with a hush. Like a secret being kept.

Her hands find the sheets, twist them. She tries to rise, to scream, but the air thickens. Her mouth shapes the sound, but it does not leave.

The demon does not rush.

It kneels beside the bed.

One hand lifts, long fingers curling inward, palm facing itself like prayer.

And from the center—

A slit. A breath. A bloom.

Bone unspools. Obsidian-black. Wet with memory. The blade does not grow so much as arrive.

It hums softly, as if recalling a song.

It leans over her. Not with cruelty. With reverence.

She kicks. Connects. The mattress shifts beneath them. The bedframe groans. A lamp falls. A drawer opens in protest. Her hand grabs for something—a pen, a ring, a pillow. Anything.

But the demon is already within reach.

It strikes.

The blade finds flesh. First across her shoulder. A carving. A sentence without language.

She screams now. The sound jagged and animal.

But she does not yield.

Not yet.

Something in her refuses. A scream twists out from deep in her chest—not sound, but will. Her hands, slick with blood, find the edge of the nightstand. The lamp crashes to the floor. She throws her weight, all of it, toward the demon. The bedframe screeches against the hardwood, half-collapsing beneath them.

And for a moment—just a breath—it stumbles.

The demon reels.

A knee drives upward. A fist lands hard against the twisted form of a jaw. Her other hand—blinded by instinct—grabs the cord of the fallen lamp and swings it wide. The base strikes the demon with a dull crack. Glass skitters across the floor.

Her voice breaks through.

A full scream now. Fierce. Risen. Shaking the corners of the room.

She lunges for the door. One foot connects with the floor, the other catches in the tangle of sheets and blood. The world lurches sideways. She slams into the dresser. Drawers burst open, contents spilling like entrails—

pens, perfume, photographs. A frame shatters.

Still she fights.

Fingernails claw at its hollow face. She bites. She kicks. Her elbow drives into its wretched form, hard enough to push the demon back.

And for one impossible instant—

The demon flickers.

The mask slips.

It reels – not in pain, but in rage.

And from somewhere deep inside its core, it lets out a sound.

A scream.

Not like a man. Not like a beast

It is a sound torn from the vaults of some ancient, starless place.

A sound with depth, not pitch – a wet groan that rises into a sharp, metallic shriek, like bone dragged across rusted iron.

It shudders through the floorboards. Sets the walls trembling.

It is not loud. Not exactly. But it fills the room.

It is the sound of mothers miscarrying in the dark.

The sound of daughters calling out from beneath the earth.

It is a sound no one survives unmarked.

She scrambles backward on hands and heels, leaving a red trail. Her palm finds a candle—thick, unused, heavy. She throws it, full force. It connects. It snarls.

The blade doesn't bloom this time.

It erupts.

No ritual. No reverence. Just fury.

It cuts through her rising arm, cleaving muscle from bone. She screams again—higher now, cracked and primal.

Another strike. Across her thigh.

Another. Across her side.

The room is chaos—bed split, walls marked, a life unraveling by the second.

But even as her body weakens, even as the blood pools fast and wide—

She glares into its face. Sunken caverns where eyes should be.

She lets it see her rage. Her refusal. Her name, still alive inside her.

The mattress now on the floor, soaked in blood. She tries to crawl. Her fingers smear crimson across the floor. Her knee catches the edge of the sheet. Her foot kicks the dresser, knocking the candle sideways.

Another cut. This time in the abdomen – a deep, clean slice. Not jagged. Not frenzied

She turns.

And still, she meets its hollow eyes.

And when she finally falls, it is not with surrender.

It is with defiance carved into the floor beneath her.

The demon watches the flicker. The slow dimming of the spark behind her gaze.

And then—

Stillness.

Not peace. Never peace.

But silence.

The body twitches once more. Reflex. Echo. The muscles do not know it is over.

But the demon does.

It does not withdraw.

It lingers.

Kneels again beside what remains—

not to mourn,

not to honor,

but to claim.

Its gnarled hands move—not in violence now,

but in possession.

Slow. Unrushed.

The way a beast returns to the place of feeding.

Or a cursed thing, compelled to caress what undoes it.

Time stretches.

Not forward.

Downward.

Inward.

The room does not breathe.

The blood does not cool.

And something far more sacred than skin begins to unravel.

If there is a god watching, it does not intervene.

Only the walls witness.

And they will not speak.

The blade retracts, folding into the wet flesh of the demon like a memory too dangerous to hold.

Something clings to its tip.

Viscous. Threaded with ruin.

It drips once –

Onto the torn cotton mattress below.

Soaks in without ceremony

A stain no one will name.

Not tonight.

Not for forty years.

It reaches forward.

Not to claim. Not to consume.

But to mark.

Its mouth—such as it is—presses against her cheek. Gently. A mockery of affection. And when it lifts away, it leaves behind a small, round burn.

The shape of a Lincoln Log.

A token.

A brand.

The room holds its breath.

The demon stands.

Blood pools beside her. Slow. Steady. The sheets are twisted. The lamp broken. The mattress angled off the frame. Her hands are still clenched.

Outside, a car passes. Headlights sweep across the closed blinds. The house does not move. The neighbors do not wake. The world continues, unaware.

The demon shudders once. Then twice.

It steps back.

Not because it must.

But because the hunger has been fed.

Not sated.

Satisfied.

It sinks away like breath returning to lungs. The skin seals. The seam disappears. Only the burn remains. Only the blood.

It slithers out the front door.

The glasses on the side table remain.

Half full.

One marked with lipstick. One not.

The night swallows it whole.

And no one sees it leave.

* * *

By dawn, the house will open again. A friend will knock. A call will go unanswered.

And the echoes of the struggle will be pieced together slowly:

The overturned mattress.

The blood.

The strange, precise burn.

The viscous drip, soaked into the mattress.

The evidence that speaks but cannot scream.

And far away, behind ribs that have closed again, the demon will sleep.

Content.

Until the hunger stirs once more.

CHAPTER 9

THE SPACE BETWEEN

Muskegon, Michigan – Late 1980

Miriam hadn't slept.

She'd tried. Listened to the steady tick of the kitchen clock, the breathing of the house, the sigh of her own lungs. But her mind would not release her.

It wasn't fear exactly. And not grief.

It was the sound of something unspoken vibrating against the walls. A low note between thought and silence. A hum, barely audible. But it was there.

The phone call had come just after dawn.

A man's voice. Flat. Bureaucratic.

He's in custody, ma'am. There was an incident. An attempted assault. Discharging a weapon. A woman was involved. We'll have more details soon.

And then the line had gone dead.

No apology. No name. No details. No mercy.

She had stared at the receiver for nearly an hour after. As if the phone itself might reverse its message. As if time might rupture and undo what had already been spoken.

But time, she was learning, did not care for hope.

Harlan was in jail.

She did not cry.

Instead, she dusted the living room twice. Windexed the hallway mirror. Scrubbed the linoleum in the kitchen with lemon water, then again with vinegar, just to be sure. Rearranged the books on the shelf alphabetically. Then by height. Then by subject. Then gave up and stacked them by color.

Now she stood in the hallway, a damp rag in her hand, staring at nothing.

The house felt hollow. Too clean. Too still.

Behind her, from Lauren's room, came the soft, irregular cadence of a child's voice. Miriam turned slightly, listening.

Lauren was speaking to her dolls.

The voice was soft, measured. Almost maternal. The tone she had once heard in department stores—young mothers murmuring to fussy babies while folding coupons into their pockets. Lauren was mimicking them perfectly.

She paused. Laughed. Whispered something only the dolls would understand.

The sound twisted something in Miriam's chest.

She wanted to walk down the hall. To kneel beside her daughter and place a hand on her small back and say: Everything is alright. Daddy just made a mistake. He'll be back soon.

But none of that felt true.

And worse, it felt known. As though the lie had already been rehearsed inside her.

She turned toward the hallway mirror.

It stood in its usual place – anchored in the wall like a memory too heavy to move.

Its glass reflected the far end of the corridor, the edge of the kitchen, and just the corner of the door to Lauren's room.

Nothing moved.

And still, she didn't like looking at it for too long.

There was something about the reflection that felt slightly delayed. As though it waited for her to look away before changing shape.

She turned instead to the bedroom. Sat on the edge of the mattress.

The house—her life—felt rearranged. As though someone had taken every object and moved it one inch to the left. Nothing dramatic. Just enough to make her unsure of where she stood.

She looked at the phone again. Then at the clock.

9:47 AM.

Time was moving. But she wasn't.

She walked outside, barefoot, down the front steps and onto the porch. The concrete was cool beneath her feet. A blue jay skittered across the fencepost. The neighbor's lawnmower buzzed faintly in the distance, a far-off hum, like a memory brushing the edge of her awareness.

She crossed her arms, more out of habit than cold.

What would she tell Lauren?

She wasn't old enough to understand jail. And Miriam wasn't ready to explain it. Not yet. Maybe not ever.

What would she tell her friends from church? Or the woman at the grocery store who always asked about Harlan's job?

What story would she tell herself?

She should have felt angry. Or afraid. Or something sharp enough to give the moment shape. But what settled into her chest instead was worse. It was the question she didn't dare speak: Had she known? Had she always known? And if so—why hadn't she stopped him?

The sun broke slightly through the trees, scattering a web of gold across the driveway. The world looked the same. But she knew it wasn't.

She turned to go back inside.

And paused.

The kitchen window was cracked open. But she hadn't left it open. She was sure.

The curtain fluttered slightly, then stilled.

Inside, a glass on the counter shifted—just slightly.

Not enough to fall.

Just enough to move.

She opened the door slowly and stepped in.

Nothing had changed.

But something had.

She placed her hand on the edge of the counter. The glass was warm to the touch.

She blinked. Told herself it was nothing. Maybe the wind.

Still, she glanced behind her. No one.

She heard Lauren laugh again. But this time, the laughter was softer. Not playful.

More like nervousness in disguise.

Miriam moved down the hall.

Lauren was sitting on the windowsill in her room, dolls lined up beside her like quiet witnesses. She wasn't speaking to them now. Just staring out the window.

"Hey, sweet girl," Miriam said.

Lauren didn't turn. But she nodded.

Miriam crossed the room slowly. Sat at the edge of the bed.

She opened her mouth to ask—what, she didn't know. But the words caught in her throat.

So she said nothing.

Lauren finally spoke. "Daddy didn't say goodbye this time."

Miriam swallowed.

"No," she said. "He didn't."

Lauren nodded, still not looking at her. "Is he coming back?"

Miriam paused. "Not for a little while."

Lauren nodded again. Her hand reached for one of the dolls. She held it tight against her chest.

Miriam stood.

"I'll make toast," she offered.

"Okay," Lauren whispered.

In the kitchen, she reached for the toaster.

Then stopped.

The photograph on the refrigerator—the one of the three of them at the beach last summer—was crooked.

She hadn't touched it.

She straightened it. But it felt wrong.

Not just tilted.

Moved.

She walked back to the bedroom and sat on the bed again.

The morning had stretched too long.

Time wasn't passing. It was hovering.

She lay back on the mattress. Closed her eyes.

And from somewhere in the house—a click.

Not the radiator. Not the pipes.

A footstep.

She sat upright.

Listened.

Nothing.

But the air had shifted.

She stood, walked to the hallway, and turned toward the mirror again.

It showed the hall, the door, the kitchen window.

And something else.

A shimmer.

Faint. Like heat rising from pavement.

Not a shape. Not a person.

But a pressure. Like someone exhaling inside her skin. Not cold. Not warm. Just... other.

She didn't move.

Didn't speak.

She only watched.

And the shimmer stilled.

As if it had been seen.

She turned. Walked away.

In the hallway behind her, the shimmer waited.

Not Temperance. Not yet.

But something adjacent to memory—something shaped like a name she hadn't remembered forgetting.

A presence held back not by time, but by will.

It would not speak yet.

It would not show itself.

But it was watching.

Waiting.

Not for vengeance.

For recognition.

CHAPTER 10:
DORMANCY

Time had stopped meaning anything reliable. Dates were assigned like stickers—neat, but never quite sticking to the truth. The light in the cell is always humming.

It doesn't flicker—it moans.

At night, it casts a faint halo across the metal sink, which never stays clean no matter how many times he wipes it down.

Harlan doesn't sleep much anymore.

Three hours, maybe four.

He lies on his side facing the wall, listening to the heat press against the concrete. Listening to the other men shifting in their bunks, coughing into the dark, whispering prayers or threats. He doesn't join them.

He counts.

Not time.

Not sins.

Something slower. Something deeper. Like the sound of a heartbeat beneath water.

In the first month, he dreamed of strange things.

A roadside.

A shape—running limbs, dark hair, a soundless scream.

He dreamed of a flicker. A hand.

He remembered a boy in the shed behind his uncle's house. Not a name. Just the sound. Just the stillness after.

He woke up soaked in sweat, the mattress peeling away from his skin.

His mouth full of rust.

He stopped dreaming after that.

Or if he did, he forgot.

Now it's just silence.

And the hum.

The mirror above the sink is dull steel, bolted down.

It does not reflect.

It remembers.

He tries not to look at it.

But sometimes, he slips.

When he's brushing his teeth or washing his hands, he catches movement that shouldn't be there.

Not a shape.

Not a face.

A shadow that bent against the light.

A pulse in the metal.

A shimmer like breath trapped behind glass.

He doesn't tell the guards.

He told the chaplain once.

The chaplain listened, then gave him a new Bible. Suggested prayer.

But Harlan's fingers burned when he held it.

He still keeps it under his cot.

He does not touch it.

Sometimes, he wakes and finds it closer to his pillow than he remembers leaving it.

It never gathers dust.

He feels it worst in the mornings.

When the light is weakest.

When the ache behind his ribs returns—not like hunger, not like heartburn, but something stranger.

A pressure.

Like his body is holding a secret it doesn't want to keep anymore.

He presses his hand to his chest sometimes, waiting for it to pass.

It never does.

The guards call him quiet.

He never causes trouble. Never complains. Eats his meals. Keeps his space clean.

They think he's getting better.

But Harlan doesn't feel better.

He feels… farther.

As though his body is a house someone else has started to live in.

The corners feel colder.

The windows rattle when there's no wind.

The floorboards creak without weight.

And sometimes, in the middle of the night, he hears something walking the halls that isn't there.

Something that breathes like memory.

He writes to Miriam every week.

He tells her things she wants to hear.

That he's reading Psalms.

That he's praying every night.

That he misses Lauren.

That he knows what he did was wrong.

That he's a better man now.

Sometimes he believes it.

Sometimes he forgets what he's apologizing for.

And sometimes, he's sure it wasn't him at all.

He signs the letters in cursive.

Underlines phrases like "God is with me."

Even when he doesn't feel it.

Even when he senses the truth beneath his ribs twisting tighter, like a chain made of breath.

There are days when the name returns to him.

Not spoken.

Not written.

Just… present.

Like the taste of metal.

Like the space between waking and sleep.

The pressure sharpens when he sees blood in the sink.

When he hears a woman's voice on the radio in the yard.

When someone walks too close behind him.

It coils.

Becomes shape.

He does not name it hunger.

He names it "the pressure."

He names it "the wound."

He names it nothing, because to name it would make it real.

Once, late in the second year, a man in the cell beside him took his own life.

Harlan heard the choking sound.

The gasping.

The final breath.

He sat on the edge of his cot.

Did not call for help.

Did not move.

The light flickered once, then steadied.

The silence that followed was deeper than the dark.

And in that hush, Harlan whispered—

"Let it in."

He did not know what he meant.

But something inside him stirred.

And smiled.

There were moments, just before sleep, when he almost spoke to it.

Not in words, but in shape—his breath forming syllables he didn't understand.

He never finished the sentence.

He didn't want to know what it might say back.

Sometimes, in the space between blinks, the sink bled.

Not red.

Not liquid.

Just... wrong.

Like something trying to remember how blood works.

The Bible never moved when he watched it.

But it was always closer.

Always there.

He does not know how long he's been waiting.

Only that time has changed shape.

Days blur.

Nights lengthen.

And the pressure never leaves.

It only coils tighter.

On the morning of his release, they give him back his watch.

He holds it in his palm.

The hands are still ticking.

The time is still wrong.

He slips it on.

And feels the cold weight settle against his wrist like a chain he asked for.

As the gate opens and the sky pours over him for the first time in years, Harlan steps forward.

And behind his ribs, something opens one eye.

It does not blink.

It does not speak.
It only waits.
And remembers.

CHAPTER 11

THE HOUSE SETTLES

Muskegon, Michigan – Spring 1982

The house had not collapsed.

That was the first surprise.

Its frame still held.

The windows opened without resistance.

The pipes clanged the same hollow notes when the heat kicked on, as if no time had passed at all.

The maple out front dropped its blossoms in delicate twirls, brushing the battered porch with pale pink confetti.

As if to reassure her:

Nothing has changed.

But it had.

Everything had.

Fifteen months since the trial.

Since the mugshot.

Since the word husband began to sound like a question in her own mouth.

Now he was home.

Harlan.

He moved through the house like furniture—solid, quiet, always somehow where she didn't expect him. He rose early and left for the hardware shop, came home with hands that smelled of rust and oil, ate without comment, slept without turning.

He hadn't touched her since the day he returned.

And she hadn't asked him to.

Some part of her still braced against the sound of his boots at the door.

Still held its breath when his keys rattled against the counter.

The walls held up, but something in her did not.

Miriam folded the laundry in silence.

Her hands moved by memory—shirt, fold, tuck, repeat. The rhythm was soothing, mechanical. She kept her eyes on the fabric, letting it blur into soft, formless color.

A flutter passed low in her abdomen.

Not a kick. Not yet.

Just a brush.

Like a moth, tapping behind her ribs.

She paused, hand resting lightly over her belly.

Her blouse was soft cotton, pale blue—the one she liked best now.

It did not cling.

The laundry basket sat at her feet. Beside it, a single pink sock. Too small to be Lauren's. Too early to have been worn.

She bent to pick it up, cradling it between her fingers.

It felt impossibly light, as if it might float away if she let go.

In the hallway, a door creaked.

Footsteps padded toward the kitchen—quick, careful.

No words.

Just the sound of a child growing older without needing to ask permission anymore.

Lauren was quiet lately.

Too quiet.

She had begun sorting her notebooks by color. Arranging her pencils in rows. Keeping her schoolbag packed by the front door days in advance.

Ten going on something older.

Something Miriam could not name.

From time to time, she caught Lauren watching her.

Not with curiosity.

With something harder.

A kind of reverence, or suspicion—as if waiting for Miriam to become something else entirely.

The doctor had said everything was normal.

Miriam had not asked about dreams.

She returned the folded clothes to the dresser drawers, moving carefully, reverently.

The nursery remained empty.

The cradle still tucked away, waiting.

Waiting until it felt safe to hope.

Later, she stood at the sink, rinsing a chipped plate.

Outside, Harlan sat on the porch, a cigarette burning between his fingers.

He did not look at the yard.

He looked through it.

Through the trees, the grass, the battered mailbox leaning on its post.

As if something might come back to claim him.

Or worse—as if something already had.

The porch light caught the smoke from his cigarette and twisted it into ghostly shapes that rose and vanished before her eyes.

Miriam turned back to the dishwater.

The curtain beside her shifted.

No breeze.

Only the house, breathing.

The mirror in the hallway caught her eye as she turned.

It had always been there – watching.

Not just hers, but her mother's, her grandmother's.

A history of women reflected, and never quite returned.

Passed hand to hand like a secret too fragile to speak aloud.

Its mahogany frame curled with fretwork, the phoenix carved in flight.

But the glass—

The glass had changed.

No longer just old, no longer just soft at edges.

Now it wavered like water.

Now it waited.

Miriam didn't look directly at it.

She let it linger in the corner of her vision –

Like something breathing just beyond.

And for a breath—only a breath—she thought she saw a figure standing just behind her reflection.

Not moving.

Not beckoning.

Only waiting.

She pressed one hand again to her stomach.

The flutter was gone.

From the end of the hall, the mirror caught the nightlight's glow, curving the soft gold into something stranger.

The light bent and breathed, as if the glass remembered a different room, a different child, a different life.

She knew that feeling.

The presence that was not a person.

The chill that came not with cold, but with memory.

Temperance.

That was the name, wasn't it?

No one had spoken it aloud in this house.

Not even the girl.

Lauren.

Who once was Elara.

Miriam had renamed her.

Had done so with trembling love.

Or need.

"Her name is Lauren now," she had said, standing on the threshold of a new life she could barely see.

And the woman at the door—Marla Keene—had nodded, as though names were just clothes to be changed.

But something had refused to forget.

* * *

That night, Miriam sat in bed, a book open on her lap, her eyes tracing the same paragraph again and again without absorbing a single word.

Across the room, Harlan sat in the chair by the window.

He did not move.

Did not turn.

The smoke from his cigarette had been replaced by the steady, hollow rhythm of his breathing.

She closed the book softly.

Listened.

The house settled around them.

Pipes groaned somewhere deep in the walls.

The maple branches rattled faintly against the siding.

Lauren's quiet breathing threaded down the hallway, steady and small.

And then—

Another sound.

Not footsteps.

Not a voice.

A shift.

A drawing inward, like the house itself holding its breath.

The flutter returned.

Sharper this time.

Miriam gasped softly, both hands flying to her belly.

It passed—but left her heart pounding against her ribs like a trapped bird.

She turned her head toward the hallway.

At the far end of the hallway, the old mirror reflected the faint glow of the nightlight.

Nothing else.

And yet—

In the curve of the old glass, the light trembled.

Shivered.

Something behind the reflection did not blink.

Did not move.

Only waited.

And remembered.

CHAPTER 12

AFTERTASTE

West Michigan – 1983

It learned patience.

Once, the hunger had risen like a storm—

all teeth and shadow and flame—

bursting through flesh, eager to rupture the skin and spill itself into the world.

But time, even to the demon, had a quieting effect.

The passage of years folded it inward.

Taught it to wait.

Taught it to listen.

Patience was not surrender.

It was preparation.

Now it moved slowly, the demon like a blade sheathed in its own heat.

It did not tremble.

It did not sing.

It watched.

The demon had evolved.

Harder.

Leaner.

More obedient.

The joints no longer protested.

The breath no longer steamed unless commanded to.

Even the heartbeat could be silenced, when silence mattered.

It did not hunt like it used to.

It did not need to.

It waited.

She left work late.

Alone.

Black flats.

Navy windbreaker.

Keys on a pink plastic ring.

The parking lot stretched wide and empty, just gravel and sodium light.

Her steps were quick, practiced.

She carried the safety of routine like a shield.

The demon admired that.

The confidence.

The complete unawareness.

It moved in the trees.

Low branches brushed its wretched face.

It did not blink.

Did not rustle.

The sky sagged with bruised cloud.

Rain threatened.

Somewhere far off, a train wailed.

She reached her car.

Fumbled for her keys.

It stepped from the trees.

No sound.

Only pressure.

Like a hole torn in the night.

She turned.

Froze.

Recognition did not come all at once.

It rippled.

A shudder.

A tremor of the old animal mind.

She tried to scream.

The sound caught in her throat.

The demon stepped closer.

Not a man.

Not quite.

A figure assembled from nightmare and suggestion.

She ran.

The blade took form in the creature's hand, curling from the palm like molten glass—a bloom of black flame edged in red.

It leapt forward.

She didn't make it far.

The gravel stole her footing.

The keys slipped from her hand.

The blade entered her cleanly.

Just above the navel.

A lover's precision.

No scream – only the soft gasp of breath caught in the throat.

Then came the draw.

No downward. Upward.

A slow, reverent unzipping –

As if the creature sought to read her.

To open her like scripture.

A glistening red bloom spilled forward – viscera unraveling in a hush, we ribbons kissing the gravel in surrender.

She swayed once,

twice,

then folded,

her body cradling itself around the hollow where life had been.

There was no rush.

No surge.

No divine flame.

Only her eyes.

Flickering.

Confused.

Then gone.

The demon stood over her, motionless.

The blade dissolved.

Its hunger, once so ravenous, offered no satisfaction.

It had fed.

But something in it remained empty.

Not hollow from starvation.

Hollow from something else.

It listened.

Not for sirens.

Not for voices.

For the feeling that had crept beneath the kill.

A shift.

A silence that wasn't empty.

The demon stepped back.

It glanced toward the trees.

The wind moved.

But nothing else.

The demon shivered.

Not from cold.

From unease.

The eyes of the woman lingered in its mind.

Wide.

Unresisting.
Not afraid enough.
Not sacred enough.
The demon had killed.
But it had not conquered.

CHAPTER 13

MIRIAM, WATCHING

Muskegon, Michigan – 1983

The baby wouldn't sleep.

Miriam rocked slowly in the glider, her heel tracing a quiet, unconscious arc across the nursery floor.

The motion was small. Habitual.

A gesture half-rooted in instinct, half in resignation.

Outside, moonlight strained through the lace curtain, casting the walls in watery shapes—soft, shifting silhouettes that moved like moths but breathed like memories.

The child stirred again.

Not crying.

Just restless.

Eyelids fluttering, lips twitching under the invisible weight of some infant dream.

Miriam shifted her hold, brushing her fingers across the child's brow.

The warmth there always surprised her—

how the skin of something so small could carry so much heat, so much proof of life, against the frailty of bone and breath.

She leaned her cheek against the baby's fine hair.

The scent was clean. Pure.

Like rain on new wood.

She closed her eyes briefly.

Let herself believe—just for a moment—that the world was smaller than it was.

Just this room.

Just this breathing.

But the house answered otherwise.

A floorboard shifted.

A pipe ticked.

The walls exhaled a breath she could not see.

Down the hall, another child moved.

Not the baby.

Lauren.

No words. No cry. Just the faint rustle of blankets, the restless shifting of a body that knew its own unease.

Miriam did not rise.

She had learned not to.

Lauren no longer wanted comfort from her.

There had been a time when the girl clung to her skirts,

reached for her hand in the parking lot,

whispered secrets into her shoulder as if the space between them was sacred.

That time had slipped away.

Miriam could not say precisely when.

Maybe after Harlan returned.

Maybe after the birth.

Maybe both.

Now Lauren closed doors with quiet finality.

Said goodnight with her back turned.

Wore her silences like armor.

Miriam shifted the baby higher on her shoulder.

The infant's breath fluttered warm against her collarbone.

Tiny hands curled like sleeping moths against her chest.

A second chance, she thought.

A chance to begin again.

To get it right.

To be the kind of mother whose voice stitched safety into dreams.

But the thought snagged on something inside her—

something that did not believe in second chances.

Something that knew what was lost could not be mended by new cloth.

Because nothing had really gone away.

Not the weight.

Not the quiet.

Not the presence she sometimes felt brushing the mirrors after dark.

Lauren had started saying strange things.

At first, Miriam dismissed them.

Children told stories.

Dreamed waking dreams.

But Lauren did not speak like a child inventing ghosts.

She reported things—

plainly, precisely—

as though taking attendance.

A woman in the hallway.

A soft knock when no one stood at the door.

Whispers after the lights went out—not words, but sounds shaped like memory.

Miriam had wanted to believe it was nothing.

But it was the way Lauren said it that unsettled her.

Not with fear.

With familiarity.

As though the presence was not an intruder, but a neighbor long since moved in.

And worse—

Lauren did not seem afraid.

Not entirely.

There was a curiosity that haunted her voice.

A knowing that went too deep for ten years old.

Miriam rose carefully from the chair, cradling the infant against her one last moment before laying her into the crib.

The girl stirred, but did not wake.

Miriam smoothed the blanket over her chest, watching the tiny ribs lift and fall in time with some unseen tide.

She stood still a moment longer, listening.

The house answered in murmurs.

Pipes settling.

Wind threading through the eaves.

The distant shifting of branches.

And then—

a sound.

Not loud.

Not sharp.

Just a tap.

One tap.

No direction.

No source.

Not on the door.

Not in the walls.

Inside.

Miriam held her breath.

Nothing followed.

No cry.

No footstep.

No excuse.

Only stillness.

She moved into the hallway.

Lauren's door was cracked.

Light spilled through in a narrow ribbon across the carpet—

not the house light.

A flashlight maybe.

Or the lamp turned too low to hold back the dark.

Miriam stood in the doorway.

Lauren sat upright on the bed.

Legs crossed.

Spine straight.

Hands resting lightly on her knees.

She was not reading.

Not playing.

Not watching anything.

She was staring.

At the wall.

Unblinking.

Miriam opened her mouth to speak.

But then she saw it.

Something shifted.

Behind Lauren.

Just past the reach of the lamp's feeble glow.

A shape.

Tall.

Indistinct.

Drifting.

Like smoke curling in reverse,

retreating upward toward the ceiling.

It moved without moving—

a suggestion more than a body.

A smudge against the certainty of the world.

Miriam blinked hard.

Gone.

The room seemed to sigh, as if in relief or exhaustion.

Her mouth stayed open a moment longer, caught between a word and its retreat.

She did not step inside.

She did not call her daughter's name.

Instead, she stepped back—

slowly, carefully—

and closed the door until only a sliver of light escaped.

"Let her be," she thought.

"Just let her be."

She turned toward her own room, heart thudding tight against her ribs.

But she did not run.

She did not pray.

She had long since stopped doing either.

The hallway stretched ahead of her, familiar and wrong all at once.

The mirror waited on the opposite wall—

the old one, brought from her mother's house,

its mahogany frame darkening with age,

the gilded phoenix at its apex tarnished to a whisper of gold.

The glass shimmered faintly, warping the light as if breathing.

And as Miriam passed, something flickered in the glass.

A shimmer.

A silhouette.

Hair like riverweed, drifting in air that did not move.

Not a woman.

Not yet.

But not gone.

Watching.

Miriam closed the door to her bedroom softly behind her.

The lock clicked into place with a sound too small to keep anything out.

She leaned against the door for a moment, her forehead resting against the wood.

Breathing.

Listening.

Down the hall, Lauren lay in her bed, eyes open in the dark.

Waiting.

For the sound to return.

CHAPTER 14

LAUREN'S EYES

Muskegon, Michigan – 1984

Lauren sat at the kitchen table, her pencil moving in slow, steady circles.

She wasn't writing.

Not really.

She was drawing.

In the center of her notebook, page after page, she sketched the same shape:

a dark, solid circle.

Black. Absolute.

No words. No lines. No borders.

Just the void.

She had started weeks ago.

At first, she hadn't even known why.

It had come to her like a memory waking from deep sleep—

not an image, but a feeling she could not place.

Now, the circle was the only thing that made sense.

The pencil worked without her really thinking about it.

The motion was soft, hypnotic.

A kind of prayer shaped in graphite.

The air in the kitchen was heavy, wet with the lingering scent of soap and boiled potatoes.

The baby gurgled softly against Miriam's hip.

Miriam stood at the sink, rinsing bottles one by one, her thoughts moving somewhere slow and unreachable.

The warm water rushed over her fingers, but it did not anchor her.

She moved like someone walking through water—thick, dream-heavy.

Behind her, the back door creaked open.

Boots thudded against the tile—heavy and deliberate.

Harlan.

"What are you doing?" he asked.

His voice was not curious.

It was flat. Expectant.

Lauren didn't answer.

Her pencil moved in its slow orbit, deeper now, grinding the graphite harder into the page.

"I said, what are you doing?"

She looked up.

Her eyes were calm.

Blank.

Unreadable.

"Homework," she said.

But she didn't flip the page.

She didn't hide it.

She didn't flinch.

Harlan stepped closer.

The kitchen light cast his shadow across the table, swallowing her hands, her notebook.

He looked down.

Saw the circle.

A small twitch moved along his jawline.

"That's not homework," he muttered.

Lauren said nothing.

The pencil hovered over the blackness, its tip trembling just slightly.

Harlan's hand came down on the table with a sharp thud.

The glass salt shaker jumped.

The baby startled, letting out a soft cry.

"Don't lie to me."

Miriam turned slightly, bouncing the baby on her hip.

"Harlan…" she said softly.

A warning.

A plea.

He ignored her.

"What is this crap?" he growled.

He grabbed the notebook, flipping through the pages roughly.

Each one revealed the same image—

the circle, again and again, relentless, deepening.

His face darkened.

"You think this is funny?

You think this is some kind of game?"

Lauren's shoulders tensed.

But she did not move.

She did not lower her eyes.

She simply watched him.

Steady.

Silent.

Something in her stillness seemed to provoke him more than any rebellion would have.

The slap came without warning.

An open palm.

A crack of skin against skin.

Lauren's head snapped sideways from the force.

Her cheek reddened almost instantly, blooming under the kitchen light.

But she did not cry out.

She held still.

Her lips pressed into a thin, bloodless line.

Miriam flinched.

The baby whimpered, clutching at Miriam's blouse with tiny, desperate fingers.

Harlan turned toward them, his face unreadable, his chest rising and falling in slow, heavy breaths.

"Control her," he said.

"Before I do."

Miriam did not speak.

She kissed the baby's temple, turned her gaze back to the sink.

The warm water ran over her hands, washing nothing clean.

Lauren wiped her cheek with the back of her hand.

Picked up her pencil again.

And turned to a new page.

The circle came easier this time.

Darker.

Deeper.

As if it were not drawn but revealed, etched beneath the surface all along.

Upstairs, a lightbulb flickered in the hallway.

The mirror shimmered, almost imperceptibly, as if remembering something it was not supposed to.

And in the silence that followed, Lauren lifted her head.

Saw something.

Not directly.

Not in the world.

But in the corner of the mirror's curve, in the soft trembling of light.

A figure.

A shape.

Not the demon.

Something else.

A woman.

Watching.

The hair floated in still air, long and dark, trailing like riverweed.

The form was indistinct, blurred at the edges like something half-remembered.

But there was no mistaking the feeling that poured from it.

Not threat.

Not malice.

Recognition.

Lauren stared back—unblinking.

The house around her seemed to fade, walls receding into shadows.

The pencil slipped from her fingers, rolling off the table and clicking against the tile.

She didn't move to retrieve it.

The woman remained.

Just for a breath.

Just long enough.

And then—

gone.

Miriam stood frozen at the sink, the water still running.

Her ears rang.

The sound of the slap still echoed against the walls of the house, louder than it had been, carrying weight beyond sound.

She turned finally.

Lauren had gone back to drawing, another circle already blooming in black graphite.

Miriam opened her mouth to speak.

Closed it again.

What could she say?

What would matter?

She pressed a kiss to the baby's hair and carried her out of the kitchen, her heart pounding in a rhythm she could not slow.

In the hallway, the mirror shivered once more.

The gilded phoenix at its crown seemed almost to bow, its tarnished wings trembling in the faint current of the unseen.

The glass breathed.

Light distorted in its surface, bending into impossible angles.

And somewhere, far beyond sight,

a tether tightened.

Not broken.

Not slack.

Pulled taut across years and grief and silence.

Waiting.

Lauren sat at the table, a new page in front of her.

The circle grew.

Wider.

Blacker.

Deeper.

And the shape in the mirror—

the watching woman—

waited, too.

CHAPTER 15

THE THRESHOLD

Muskegon, Michigan – 1985

Lauren had stopped speaking much at home.

Not out of protest, nor fear. Not even habit. It was quieter inside her now, as if something sacred had wrapped itself around her thoughts and asked for silence. Not secrecy. Stillness. A quiet so complete it felt like water—cool and enclosing, distorting voices and slowing movement.

Each night, she lay in bed with the notebook pressed to her chest. The pages had grown heavy with graphite, the circles deeper, wider, darker. Sometimes, she imagined a name no one had ever called her. Something soft. Something distant. A name she could carry somewhere else – past Michigan, past memory. If she could walk away, she would go where no one asked who she had been. She would start new. Whole. She had stopped trying to explain them even to herself. They weren't drawings. They weren't art. They were something else.

Messages, maybe.

Or doors.

That evening, the house breathed around her in its usual hush. Pipes ticked. The refrigerator hummed. Her baby sister gurgled softly in the next room. Miriam hummed a half-forgotten lullaby, out of tune and distant. Lauren lay on her back, watching the ceiling absorb the pale spill of moonlight. Her fingers toyed with the edge of the notebook.

The mirror on the wall—the old one, caught a fragment of that same moonlight. It shimmered slightly. Warped. As though the glass were moving, breathing.

Lauren sat up.

The air in the room felt heavier. Not cold. Just... expectant.

Then, in the curve of the mirror, a shape began to form. A shimmer, soft and colorless, like dust swirling through water. Hair drifted as if caught in a current. A face emerged, not quite clear, as if half in shadow and half in memory.

Temperance.

She did not speak. But her gaze—calm, aching—settled over Lauren like a blanket drawn over trembling shoulders.

Lauren crawled to the edge of the bed. Her toes found the cool wood floor. The air pressed gently against her chest.

She moved toward the mirror.

Not rushed. Not afraid.

Temperance raised one hand.

Fingers long. Familiar. As if Lauren had held them once in a dream she couldn't recall. The gesture was simple, but weighted: palm out, steady, not beckoning but grounding.

A voice—not a sound, but a certainty—moved inside Lauren:

Tell them.

Lauren blinked. Her throat tightened.

She knew what Temperance meant.

The nights.

The locked door.

The bruises that bloomed too easily.

The way Harlan looked at her sometimes. The way her mother looked away.

Temperance's image shimmered once, like a stone breaking the surface of water. Then it receded.

The mirror stilled.

Lauren remained where she was for a long time, staring at her own reflection, not sure who she was seeing.

* * *

Muskegon, Michigan – December 1987

The room smelled faintly of popcorn and the kind of fruity body spray only middle school girls wore with sincerity. Lauren sat on the floor in her best friend Abby's basement, knees drawn up, her oversized sweatshirt swallowing most of her frame. The TV buzzed low in the background—an old episode of *The Facts of Life*, neither of them had paid attention.

Abby lay belly-down on her bed, chin resting on a pink pillow. A bowl of M&Ms sat between them, untouched.

Outside, snow clicked softly against the windowpane. Inside, the light from a string of star-shaped fairy lights flickered in uneven pulses, casting shadows that danced across the posters taped to the walls.

"You've been quiet all night," Abby said finally, voice low.

Lauren shrugged.

"I'm fine."

Abby didn't push. Not yet.

A beat passed.

Then another.

Lauren picked at a bedazzled jewel on *My Little Pony* sweatshirt , fingers worrying it loose. Her voice, when it came, was almost too soft to hear.

"My dad comes into my room."

Abby blinked. "What do you mean?"

Lauren shook her head quickly, but the words kept coming, like water pressing through a crack in glass. Tears began flowing.

"Not to tuck me in. Not to say goodnight. He just… stands there. Sometimes he sits on the edge of the bed. Sometimes he touches my back. He says it's nothing, but it doesn't feel like nothing. And then he…."

Silence.

Then Abby sat up, legs swinging over the side of the bed. Her voice was cautious, but steady.

"Have you told your mom?"

"She knows," Lauren said. The words were flat. Final.

"She doesn't stop him?"

Lauren shook her head.

Abby reached out, placed a hand gently over Lauren's.

"You should tell a teacher."

"They won't believe me."

"Why not?"

"Because he goes to church. Because he makes pancakes at the monthly church Saturday breakfast."

Abby's grip tightened. "I believe you."

Lauren's eyes filled, but she blinked the tears back.

"Thanks."

They didn't say anything else. Just sat there, side by side on the soft pink carpet, while the movie flickered and the snow kept falling outside. Abby didn't let go of her hand.

Lauren sat on the edge of the edge of the couch. Abby had fallen asleep on the floor. She too her notebook our of her backpack and held it in her lap. The pages were blank. Her pencil hovered but didn't move.

She could feel it again.

The presence.

Not her father. Not exactly.

Something else.

The old golden framed mirror across the room shimmered faintly. A flicker in the glass. Not movement. Not light. Something between.

She stood.

Walked toward it.

The glass was cool beneath her fingers.

Her reflection looked back, but the eyes were wrong.

Older. Sadder. Watching.

A whisper rose behind her ears, inside her skin:

Tell them.

Lauren turned away.

She didn't draw that night.

She didn't sleep.

* * *

She told Mrs. Brandt first.

Her teacher.

It was Monday after the sleep over. The light outside was dull and snow was in the air. Lauren sat with her hands folded tightly in her lap, Abby sat next to her. Mrs. Brandt had just asked them to free write, but Lauren hadn't moved.

"Lauren?"

The girl looked up.

And then, in a voice so quiet the heater almost swallowed it, she said:

"My dad hurts me."

Mrs. Brandt blinked.

Lauren didn't elaborate.

Didn't cry.

She just repeated it.

"He touches me. He hurts me. Sometimes at night. Sometimes when I'm in the bathroom. Sometimes..."

Her voice cracked then, just once.

Mrs. Brandt stood slowly and crossed the room. She knelt down beside her.

"Okay," she whispered. "Okay. You did the right thing."

That afternoon, Lauren stayed in the school counselor's office. A woman named Janet with soft hands and glass earrings offered her cocoa and a coloring book. They didn't speak much. Lauren didn't want to answer more questions yet. But she drank the cocoa. And when Janet reached across the table and held her hand, Lauren let her.

* * *

Harlan found out that night.

No one told him directly. But someone had called the house.

A brief message.

A courtesy.

Just enough to light the match.

Miriam was the one who answered.

Lauren was upstairs.

Harlan walked in just as Miriam hung up. Her face had gone a strange color, pale but blotched at the cheeks.

"Who was it?" he asked.

She didn't answer right away.

He stepped closer.

"Who was it, Miriam?"

"Someone from the school."

She didn't meet his eyes.

"Said Lauren said some things. About you."

Harlan didn't speak for a moment.

The air in the kitchen seemed to thicken, as if it knew what was coming and wanted to cushion it.

"What things."

"I don't know," Miriam said quickly. "They didn't say."

But she knew.

She had seen the bruises.

He stepped past her, his boots loud against the linoleum.

"Harlan..."

He paused.

"Don't."

His voice was low.

Flat.

It didn't belong to him anymore.

He went upstairs.

Miriam didn't follow.

* * *

Lauren sat in her room, notebook in her lap.

The circle had returned—

darker now.

Not rage.

Not fear.

A stillness so complete it might have been peace.

She didn't look up when the door opened.

Didn't flinch.

Her pencil moved in slow, steady arcs.

And in the mirror, behind her shoulder,

Temperance watched.

Not intervening.

Not yet.

But near.

Very near.

Lauren pressed the pencil harder into the page.

The circle bled into the paper like oil.

She would not sleep that night.

And neither would the thing in the dark.

* * *

At the mirror in the hallway, Temperance placed one hand against the glass. Her outline grew clearer, her hair floating gently around her shoulders, her eyes dark with warning.

She had tried to guide.

She had tried to protect.

But time was short.

And her reach, even now, was not enough.

She whispered something against the pane—

a name—

a prayer—

a warning.

The glass held her voice like breath trapped in ice.

Lauren, turned toward the hallway.

She couldn't hear the words.

But she knew what they meant.

Run.

Hide.

He is coming.

* * *

The house did not sleep.

Not that night.

CHAPTER 16

THE DISAPPEARANCE

Rockweiller Home, Michigan – March 1989

This was the moment the story circled from the future to the beginning. But even then, no one knew it had already ended.

The house did not scream.

It listened.

The wind moved through the trees outside like breath drawn over bone. Cold, thin, endless. Upstairs, a bedroom window had been cracked open—just enough to let the air slip in and make the curtains whisper against the glass like the hems of funeral veils.

Below, the furnace stirred, then fell silent again, unsure of itself. Floorboards shifted. Pipes ticked like the metronome of something dying slowly. The refrigerator hummed its tired song in the kitchen. The soup on the stove had begun to burn, blackening around the edges, forgotten by the one who left it behind.

Miriam had gone. Just for a night. A neighbor had offered to host the younger daughter for a sleepover—an ordinary kindness in a world starved of them. She had packed the bag quickly, left a note near the stove, scrawled a rushed instruction:

Heat low. Eat something.

She hadn't noticed that Lauren had not said goodbye.

Now, the house exhaled once more. And waited.

* * *

Lauren sat cross-legged on the floor of the upstairs craft room—once a family project space, now quietly hers. The notebook was open across her lap. The circle was there again. Dark. Perfect. Endless. A mouth with no tongue. A moon with no light.

She was not drawing it anymore.

She was watching it.

The graphite had thickened to the point of rupture, layers compressed into something that absorbed rather than reflected the dim light around it. It pulsed faintly, not with movement but with memory. As if it remembered every finger that had shaped it, every silence that had clung to its making.

Her breathing was shallow. Measured. Like someone practicing death.

She had told the truth. To someone. Maybe to a teacher. Maybe to a friend. The words had fallen from her mouth like stones she could no longer carry—simple, unadorned:

He hurts me.

He touches me.

It isn't right.

And someone had listened. Or tried.

But the house knew what had been said. The walls had absorbed it. And deeper still, the thing that lived behind the man had heard it, too.

* * *

In the garage, something stirred.

It did not uncoil. It did not roar. It rose like something returning to ritual.

The demon had known many names for hunger, but none for grief. It had watched her, this changeling child, for months. Something inside her had grown inward, had darkened into knowledge. And tonight—tonight, it could feel her stillness as a kind of offering.

It did not resist.

The door opened without sound. The creature entered the house the way rot enters wood—quiet, inevitable.

It did not call her name.

It did not need to.

It ascended the stairs, each step measured, deliberate. The air thickened around it, as if the house recognized what was coming and could not bear to witness.

As it passed the hallway mirror, the glass rippled. A shimmer. A sigh. Temperance appeared there, faint as breath on silver, her eyes wide with the stillness of oceans. But she did not intervene.

Not yet.

* * *

Lauren rose to her feet as the door opened. She did not startle.

The creature entered the room like smoke, folding the shadows around itself, the scent of rust and bone thickening the air.

They faced one another.

The girl. The demon. The wound and the blade.

Lauren's voice, when it came, was quiet. Calm. Hollowed by the weight of what she already knew.

"Are you going to kill me now?"

No accusation. No plea. Only inevitability.

The demon paused.

Its body did not answer, but the blade did.

The hand split slowly. Deliberately. Bone peeled back like the petals of a black lily. From within, the weapon emerged—not summoned but birthed. A filament of shadow, pulsing red at its edge, alive with ancient flame.

Lauren tilted her head.

"She's watching you," she said.

A tremor passed through the room.

The demon hesitated. Just for a moment. Enough.

Lauren turned and ran.

* * *

The hallway stretched before her like a throat sealed in silence.

Her socks slipped on the polished wood. Her hand grazed the railing. Behind her, the air pulsed with heat. It followed.

She made it halfway down the stairs.

Behind her, the air shuddered.

The creature did not walk.

It lifted.

Weightless and obscene,

it hovered above the steps like ash caught in wind,

its form smudging the edges of the world.

And then it lunged.

The blade bloomed mid-flight—

a sudden petal of black flame,

whispering forward with terrible grace.

It struck her between the shoulder blades.

Clean. Precise.

Not a slash—

a piercing.

A kiss of steel through breath and spine.

The point buried deep,

cutting through muscle and lung,

rupturing the great vein beneath—

the vena cava—

and with it, her last warmth.

Her body seized—

a marionette yanked by an invisible thread.

Air fled her lungs in a sharp, crimson gasp.

She stumbled.

Tumbled.

The blade pulled free as she fell—

a ribbon of red spiraling behind her.

She struck the base of the stairs headfirst—

a wet, unnatural crack.

Her neck twisted sharply to one side,

chin tilted as if listening for something she would never hear.

Silence followed.

Complete.

Cathedral-like.

The demon landed softly at the top of the stairs,

its blade retracting in a shimmer of heat.

Below, her body lay crumpled at the base of the staircase—

arms bent beneath her,

hair splayed across the tile like ink in water.

A pool formed slowly beneath her ribs,

dark and pulsing.

Her eyes were still open.

* * *

The house did not wail.

But it recoiled.

The lightbulb in the hallway flickered and died. A door somewhere
upstairs slammed without touch. The mirror cracked along one edge,

hairline and shining.

The demon stood above her.

The blade vanished, dissolving into the palm with a hiss.

Lauren's body lay twisted. One arm pinned beneath her. Her hair fanned outward like black thread pulled from the spool.

The hunger stirred. But it did not swell. There was no surge of triumph. No rapture.

Only quiet.

Only a question:

Why doesn't it feel like before?

The demon crouched. Watched her chest. Waited for breath.

None came.

It reached out. Touched her cheek.

Warm.

But fading.

Something cracked beneath its ribs. A soundless rupture.

Not grief. Not quite.

But the beginning of an absence it could not name.

* * *

It lifted her.

She weighed nothing. Or too much.

Her limbs hung wrong. Her hair clung to her cheek in a wet tangle. One sock had slipped halfway off.

It held her like a father might. Like a priest. Like a sinner carrying the relic he had just defiled.

From the end of the hallway, the mirror shimmered.

Temperance appeared.

Not in rage.

But in mourning.

Her eyes did not accuse.

They bore witness.

The house held its breath.

The air turned colder.

The swing set in the backyard rocked once.

The soup boiled dry, the bottom of the pot blistering with black.

And the demon stood there, holding the girl who had named it.

* * *

The front door opened. Not wide. Just a breath of wood on metal. A draft.

And toward the woods, the demon moved with Lauren.

It passed unseen beneath the eaves, between tree and fence, between heaven and earth.

Away from house – carrying her body.

And toward the breaking.

Toward the moment the story ceased to be quiet.

Lauren's eyes remained open.

And the house, long silent, remembered how to mourn.

This was not a disappearance.

It was a rupture.

And the reckoning had already begun.

CHAPTER 17:
FILED AWAY

Rockweiller Home, Michigan – Morning After

Miriam woke before the sun.

She did not sit up.

She did not reach for the clock.

She stared at the line where ceiling met wall, waiting for it to move.

The world felt thinner in the morning.

Like it hadn't put all its weight back on yet.

Beside her, the bed was empty.

Harlan had already risen.

That wasn't unusual.

He was always up before her—

tinkering,

cleaning,

walking the property in slow, pointless loops.

Sometimes, she imagined he never slept at all.

From the other bedroom, her youngest daughter's breathing threaded gently through the wall—

soft and slow.

But from Lauren's room—

nothing.

Not quiet.

Empty.

She rose without slippers.

The cold bit at her soles like something unspoken.

Down the hallway, Lauren's door stood ajar.

A line of air moved through it—cold, careful.

She knocked, out of habit.

Or guilt.

The knock made no sound.

It vanished into the stillness like a voice swallowed by snow.

She opened the door.

The bed was made.

Not perfectly.

But carefully—

the way Lauren did everything now.

Neat edges. Taut corners.

The pillow smooth.

Her backpack sat by the chair.

Zipped. Ready.

The window was open a few inches.

The curtain breathed in and out, as if the room still lived.

Miriam stepped inside.

The room smelled of fabric softener and graphite.

But something else lingered—

a note of emptied air.

A hush not made by silence but by removal.

She found the letter on the desk.

Folded once.

The paper was thick. Her daughter's.

She reached out—

then drew back.

She already knew.

In the kitchen, the smell of coffee filled the air.

Bitter. Grounding.

But it did not feel like morning.

It felt like after.

Harlan entered from the garage.

His boots were clean.

His hands empty.

His face blank.

He kissed her cheek the way he always did—

an ordinary gesture so precise it could only be rehearsed.

"She's gone," he said.

Miriam nodded.

She didn't ask who.

"She took some money," he added, almost helpfully.

"And her things."

The words landed gently.

Like a snowflake hiding a stone.

* * *

That afternoon, Miriam sat in a plastic chair under the buzzing lights of the county sheriff's office.

The waiting room smelled of wet wool and burnt coffee.

The desk sergeant clicked his pen twice before looking up.

"Name?"

She told him.

"Your daughter ran away?"

Miriam nodded.

"Packed a few things," she murmured.

"Age?"

"Fourteen."

He gave a practiced sigh.

"She'll turn up. They always do."

A clipboard was produced.

A form handed over.

A cheap pen pressed into her palm.

In a side room, a female detective lingered at a desk.

Sergeant Rosa Daniels.

She watched Miriam through the half-open door.

Her instincts twitched—

but not enough.

Three days later, at the high school, Counselor Janine Keller sat at her desk reviewing quarterly reports.

She paused on one file.

Lauren Rockweiller.

She'd flagged it once.

There had been… indicators.

Withdrawn behavior.

Marks Lauren hadn't wanted to explain.

And that one moment in her office—

when Lauren's voice had dropped into something far too steady for a girl her age.

"He comes into my room sometimes," she'd said.

Then:

"But it's fine now. I think it's over."

Janine had reported it.

Quietly.

Internally.

No one followed up.

The Rockweillers were "a decent family."

Harlan was "strict, but solid."

She stared at the file.

Still open.

Miriam had checked the box for "runaway."

No note was included in the case folder.

Janine's hand hovered over the phone.

Then moved away.

She closed the file.

Filed it.

Away.

Miriam found the envelope two weeks later.

It had fallen behind the cabinet in the kitchen.

Inside were three twenties.

Sixty dollars Lauren had supposedly taken when she ran away.

Miriam stood staring at them for a long time.

She did not cry.

She did not tell Harlan.

She tucked the money inside a book on the shelf.

Pressed the cover closed.

Said nothing.

Some truths, she had learned, must be buried like bones—

not because they are shameful,

but because speaking them would destroy the walls of the world.

The house changed.

Subtly.

The laundry room door would no longer latch.

The baby monitor sometimes crackled even when unplugged.

The light in the upstairs hallway flickered like a heartbeat.

Miriam did not investigate.

She moved through the house like a visitor in a museum of grief.

She never reopened Lauren's door.

In the hallway mirror, a handprint appeared.

Small. Faint.

Pressed in warmth, not blood.

Left by love, not fear.

Temperance watched through the silvered glass.

She hovered now in photographs, in doorknobs, in the shimmer of spoons left too long in sunlight.

Her presence moved like static between worlds.

She did not scream.

But she remembered.

She knew the note was not written by Lauren.

She knew the lie that passed from father to mother to sheriff's station.

She knew the face of the man who walked the property at dawn, humming.

The house did not cry out.

But it listened.

And in the basement—

beneath the furnace hum—

the air thickened.

Something ancient began to stir.

Not rage.

Not yet.

Memory.

Coiling.

Growing teeth.

In the police archives, the case file for Lauren Rockweiller was marked:

MISSING – PRESUMED RUNAWAY.

No further action.

No warrant.

No press.

No one searched the woods.

No dogs.

No flyers.

Just ink.

Just paper.

Just filing.

Outside the house, a wind moved through the trees.

The swing set did not move.

In the garage, a light flickered and went out.

And from the woods beyond the fence, something watched the house with a mother's patience.

With a memory sharper than knives.

Temperance did not weep.

She waited.

For grief to ripen into fury.

For memory to take shape.

For the lie to break its own spine.

CHAPTER 18:
THE CARVING

Michigan – The Night of The Demon

"He that diggeth a pit shall fall into it."
– Ecclesiastes 10:8

The garage door hung crooked on its rail, as if it had been wrenched open by some ancient force too large for the frame. A single moth danced in the cone of light overhead, orbiting the bare bulb like it were a sun in some distant and lesser universe. And through the crooked opening, it came— stepping silently from the breathless hush of the woods, the thing that bore her.

She was slack in its arms. A girl once. A daughter. All the weight of her now no more than a cooled ember, extinguished. The demon carried her as though cradling the very idea of stillness. Her hair clung to its forearm, soaked. Her mouth, a soft parting. Her throat, dark.

It did not look down.

It did not need to.

The thing in the garage had already known her, long before she had been named.

115

The garage was cold and distant.
Concrete.
Oil.
The scent of rust and old wood.
The air inside did not move.
It shivered with absence.
The overhead light buzzed once—
faint, irregular—
then steadied into a dull, sickly glow.
The workbench stood in the center,
islanded by darkness.
Upon it, the demon lay the body.
There was no reverence in the placement.
A single hair tie lay forgotten beneath the bench—pink, with a cracked cartoon charm. Untouched by blood. Yet screaming all the same.
The demon stirred.
The hunger did not throb.
It did not shriek.
It pulsed.
A low, steady rhythm—
like breath pulled through a hollow tree.
Ancient.
Patient.
Undeniable.
Her eyes, half-lidded now, still held the glimmer of recognition – flickering death like a candle that would not go quietly.
Inside the demon, something unfolded.
The wretched skin parted willingly—
the sternum yawning open like a gate long unused.
The ribs sighed aside.
The lungs surrendered.
The demon slipped forward,

sheathed in its own inevitability.

It hovered beside her.

There were no words.

No prayers.

No invocations of forgiveness.

Only the sound of fingers against cloth,

against flesh,

against the threshold between forgetting and remembering.

The blade came forth from the center of its palm.

Not with urgency.

With gravity.

It grew—

twisted—

bone blackened by memory and marinated in centuries of hunger.

Flesh calcified into a crooked edge.

A relic.

A weapon.

A hymn.

It hummed in the cold, empty air.

And then it began.

Not out of malice.

Not for pleasure.

But because it believed—

this was the way to make her disappear.

Piece by piece.

As if she had never lived.

As if she had never looked back at it without fear.

As if mercy were a lie it could finally carve away from memory.

The blade touched her gently first.

A graze against fabric.

Then deeper.

There was no scream.

Only the soft tearing of cotton.

The slow give of skin beneath pressure.

The edge of innocence peeled back beneath the descent of something older than sin itself.

It was not pleasure.

It was dominion.

    Silence made permanent.

The demon held her while it carved.

Careful.

Precise.

Arms.

Legs.

Chest.

It could not name the feeling that rose when the blade touched her sternum – not hunger, not hate. Something else. Something dangerous.

The blade moved not like a butcher's,

but like a mortician's—

a scribe recording a death that could not be spoken.

Each stroke was deliberate.

Measured.

A mortician with no audience.

A god with no gospel.

The work was methodical, almost reverent.

The room filled not with noise,

but with the heavy, sacred sound of a life being erased.

When it was done,

the parts were wrapped.

Layered in thick black bags.

Sealed in layers of plastic.

The blood soaked into the folds—

but did not spread.

The floor stayed clean.

Almost... resistant.

As if the house itself refused to absorb it.

As if the earth was not ready yet.

The body became fragments.

The fragments became cargo.

The barrel waited against the far wall.

Steel.

Rust-ringed.

Silent.

It opened without protest.

The bags were lowered inside—

one after another,

nested carefully,

weighted down.

The lid was wired shut.

Not marked with a name.

Only weight.

Only silence.

Above, in the hallway, the light flickered once.

Then again.

Not with electricity.

With memory.

The demon settled.

Its blade retracted into flesh,

folding itself into bone.

The hunger dimmed.

But something else bloomed in its place.

Something colder than fire.

Older than guilt.

Something sacred.

Desecration.

A desecration so profound it left a mark—

not just on the body.

Not just on the soul.

On the shape of the world itself.

The demon had killed before.

But this—

this was different.

This was a forgetting made flesh.

An erasure carved into the living grain of the earth.

And desecration does not vanish.

It lingers.

It stains.

It sings.

Outside, the woods stood silent.

The wind did not move through the trees.

The swing set in the yard hung motionless.

And deep beneath the skin of the soil,

the ground had already begun to open.

Quietly.

Lovingly.

Ready to remember what the world would try to forget.

CHAPTER 19:
THE MOVE

Hamilton, Michigan – Weeks Later

Miriam folded shirts slowly.

Not to pack them.

Not yet.

Just to touch them.

The cotton had worn thin in places, made soft by years of water and warmth. A few stitches along the neckline had unraveled—small, ghostly threads curling loose like they had nowhere left to hold.

She traced one gently with her thumb.

The motion felt almost reverent.

Outside, the moving truck idled in the driveway, its engine low and steady, a mechanical breath exhaled across the thinning lawn.

Harlan passed the window—carrying boxes, shifting weight. Tools. Linens. The last things they hadn't given away or hidden in the attic.

He moved like a man enacting a task already rehearsed. Like the rhythm itself would save him.

They weren't moving far.

Just a few blocks.

Still in town.

Still close enough to drive past the old house if they wanted to.

But Miriam didn't want to.

She stood in the master bedroom, folding the shirts again.

Not to pack them.

Not yet.

Each fold came slowly. Deliberately.

She had told herself it was just to keep her hands busy.

But her hands remembered more than her mouth would say.

The photos were gone from the walls now.

The swing in the yard had been taken down.

The patch of garden Lauren used to water was already overgrown.

No one asked about the girl.

Not the neighbors.

Not the mailman.

Not even the younger daughter, who now sat on the living room floor hugging a stuffed rabbit until its fur curled between her fingers.

She looked up.

"Are we taking the garden?"

Her voice was too steady for a child.

Miriam crouched beside her.

"We'll plant a new one."

The words came easily.

As if they'd always been true.

As if you could carry roots like furniture.

The girl nodded.

Then hugged the rabbit tighter.

Miriam had tried, once, to tell her a story.

A lie sweetened at the edges.

"She left, baby. She needed time."

The child had only nodded.

As if she too understood what adults meant when they lied quietly.

Harlan's footsteps came down the hall.

"Garage is next," he said, wiping his forehead with the back of his hand, like sweat could explain the gravity in the air.

Miriam did not answer.

He moved past her and into the mouth of the garage.

The door swung shut with a sound like a breath being held.

The house did not protest.

She walked to the kitchen window.

The light outside was pale—spring-thin. The trees hadn't quite filled in, and the yard looked raw without them.

A shovel stood propped against the fence.

Its blade was dull with dried earth.

She didn't remember the last time it had been used.

Or who had used it.

She watched it for a long time.

Not thinking.

Not searching.

Just watching.

The wind moved through the trees.

The faucet dripped once.

Then twice.

She blinked.

Upstairs, a light flickered in the hallway.

A stutter.

A breath caught.

She waited.

It did not flicker again.

Back outside—between the fence and the trees—

something stood.

A figure.

Still.

Hair drifting behind it like it floated underwater.

She didn't look away.

She didn't open the door.

The figure vanished.

Not into the trees.

Into knowing.

The kind of knowing that leaves heat in its absence.

She turned from the window.

In the younger daughter's room, she folded another shirt.

A drawer stood open beside her, empty.

A photograph sat facedown on the desk.

Not missing—placed.

A mercy.

She did not turn it over.

The shirts went into a box.

No label.

No tape.

Just memory, tucked between cardboard flaps.

The floor creaked as she rose.

Not loudly.

A subtle complaint in the bones of the house.

She stepped into the hallway.

The mirror still hung crooked.

Miriam didn't look directly at it.

But she felt its weight.

The way it seemed to hold its breath when she passed.

A glimmer caught the edge of her vision.

Just the sun, maybe.

Just a shift in light.

Still, she unhooked the mirror.

Wrapped it.

Carried it.

It would go with them.

Outside, Harlan called from the truck.

She did not answer.

Not yet.

She stepped into Lauren's room—

though it no longer looked like hers.

The mattress was bare.

The closet empty, save for a single pair of shoes.

Buckled.

Shined.

Miriam didn't take them.

Some things do not want to be carried.

She lifted the wrapped mirror.

Carried it to the truck.

The grass bent beneath her steps.

Not freshly mowed.

Not wild.

Something in between.

She did not look back.

Not at the shovel.

Not at the place where the watcher had stood.

She placed the mirror carefully among the boxes.

Turned toward the house.

Its windows watched her.

The glass reflected only sky.

But she knew better.

The faucet would keep dripping.

And the house—

the house would wait.

Not haunted.

Not cursed.

But hollowed.

CHAPTER 20

THE BURIAL

New Rockweiller Home, Hamilton, Michigan – Spring 1989

The new house didn't creak the same way.

It was too clean.

Too still.

Like it hadn't yet learned how to hold secrets.

Miriam stood at the kitchen sink, holding a damp plate in one hand.

But she wasn't washing it.

Her gaze drifted to the backyard, where the morning light lay thin across the frost-hardened grass.

The sky was soft—

pale blue,

the kind that promised warmth but hadn't delivered it yet.

At the edge of the tree line,

Harlan was digging.

Not hurriedly.

Not angrily.

Methodically.

The shovel moved with a calm rhythm, as if each strike into the earth was a word in a language only he could speak.

Beside him, a blue barrel leaned against the fence—

dented, streaked with old mud,

the kind of object that was meant to be ignored.

Another barrel sat nearer the shed, sealed tightly with rusted wire.

Miriam had seen them before.

Not often.

Once or twice, tucked away in corners of garages,

beside workbenches,

beneath the weight of forgetting.

He hadn't said what they were for.

She hadn't asked.

The plate in her hand slipped slightly.

She tightened her grip.

Set it down on the towel with care.

Behind her, the younger girl played on the carpet,

dragging plastic animals into a careful line across the baseboard.

She hummed under her breath—

tuneless, steady.

Didn't look up.

Outside, the shovel struck earth again.

A pause.

Another strike.

The rhythm was calm.

Like a metronome set to something inevitable.

Miriam turned from the window.

Opened a cupboard.

Stared at the neat rows of bowls and plates,

waiting for them to tell her what to do next.

Outside, the wind shifted.

She turned back.

The yard was still.

But Harlan was gone from view.
Only the shovel remained—
its handle leaning against the fence,
its blade buried in a heap of dark, upturned soil.
The barrel had disappeared.
The ground where it had stood looked... ordinary.
Too ordinary.
Smoothed over like the closing of an eyelid.
A flicker caught her eye.
At the edge of the trees.
A figure.
Still.
Watching.
Long hair drifted around her shoulders, though the air was still.
Miriam blinked.
Gone.
Only the birches,
the pines,
the long grass leaning toward the fence.
She exhaled through her nose.
Pressed her hand to her belly without thinking.
Nothing there now.
Just muscle and bone.
But sometimes the ghost of weight still lingered.
Behind her, the younger girl giggled.
A bird flew past the window.
The ground outside seemed to settle itself deeper into the earth.
And Miriam, moving slowly,
picked up the plate again.
Not to clean it.
Just to feel the weight of something she could still hold.

* * *

Evening — Later That Day

The dishes were put away.

The carpet vacuumed.

The girl was asleep upstairs, her breath soft against the hush of her pillow.

Harlan had taken a beer out back at dusk and had not returned.

Miriam stood at the base of the stairs.

Listening.

The house was so new it hadn't yet learned how to murmur properly.

The silence felt different here.

Tight.

Held.

Waiting.

At the top of the stairs hung the mirror.

The old one.

The heirloom.

She had carried it herself—wrapped in a wool blanket from the cedar chest, sealed at the corners, unwrapped with quiet hands on the first night they moved in.

Hung it again with care.

Not out of sentiment.

Out of obligation.

Or perhaps guilt.

It sat wrong on the wall—tilted just slightly. The frame still tarnished, the curve at the bottom right still warped.

The mirror reflected only the hallway behind her.

At first.

Then—

something.

Not a face.

129

Not a shape.

Not even light.

A pulse.

A pressure behind the glass.

The mirror did not shimmer.

It breathed.

She stared.

The mahogany frame caught her reflection in uneven pieces—

her throat, her jaw, her left eye caught at an angle.

The gilded phoenix at the top – its wings dulled to a whisper of gold –
seemed to tilt forward, as if bowing to something unseen.

The glass looked back at her like it was trying to remember.

And for a moment—just long enough to draw breath—

something shifted.

Not a ghost.

Not yet.

But the hint of one.

Waiting.

Not haunting the house.

Coming with them.

Through the mirror.

Through the weight of memory still caught between glass and
reflection.

Miriam did not touch it.

She turned away.

And walked back down the stairs.

The house did not groan.

It waited.

CHAPTER 21

THE FAILED HAUNTING

Hamilton, Michigan – Late 1990

Temperance had learned the shape of the walls.

She no longer slipped between them.

She passed through.

The house, once resistant, had softened around her.

The air recognized her.

The floorboards remembered.

Even the dust curled toward her like something ashamed.

But the demon did not.

The demon—

this creature, this thing,

this skin that wore hunger like a second soul—

remained closed.

Still.

Sealed.

He moved through the house as though nothing beneath his flesh had ever stirred.

Both supernatural beings now brooded in the same space—

haunting the same hollowed corridors.

The Demon and The Woman.

A war without battlefield or banner.

A siege fought in the silence between dreams.

Temperance had tried to reveal herself.

Her remembering.

Flickers in mirrors.

Hairline fractures along window glass.

Soft raps behind the drywall where no hand should reach.

She had stood at the foot of their bed—

tall, cold, draped in sorrow,

a weight without sound.

She had poured her presence like fog into the closets,

under the beds,

through the vents.

She had waited.

And waited.

But they never woke.

Or worse—

when they did,

they only turned deeper into their sleep,

pulled the blankets higher,

retreated into the soft, safe void of forgetting.

As if forgetting could save them.

As if silence could absolve them.

But tonight, she would try again.

Tonight, she would stretch closer.

The younger daughter lay tangled in sleep,

mouth parted slightly,

one hand clutching the frayed ear of a stuffed rabbit.

Her breath rose and fell with innocent rhythm.

But her lids twitched.

Her brow tensed.

Somewhere deep in her dreams,

she stirred.

The blood remembered even when the mind denied.

Miriam had gone to bed early.

The smell of potluck casseroles and perfumed handshakes still clung to her hands.

The kind of night built on polite lies.

Her smile had been a costume all day.

Now she curled in the dark,

knees drawn toward her chest,

as if bracing for storms she could no longer name.

The house was still.

Breathless.

Waiting.

Temperance stood in the hallway, just beyond their door.

The brass knob caught the moonlight and twisted it into a crooked gleam.

She raised a hand.

Pressed her palm to the wood.

It should have groaned.

The lock should have faltered.

The latch should have whispered her name.

But nothing happened.

She pressed harder.

A light buzzed overhead.

Flickered.

Then stilled.

Temperance stepped through.

The wood passed over her like smoke.

Inside, the bedroom smelled of dust and sleep.

The air had gone stale from years of unsaid things.

Harlan lay closest to the door, turned toward the wall.
Miriam curled beside him,
one hand resting over her stomach,
as if remembering the daughters she could no longer reach.
The bedsheet rose and fell with their shallow breathing.
Temperance moved to the edge of the bed.
She leaned down, close.
And whispered.
Not in words.
Not in sound.
But in memory.
The crack of bone.
The soft collapse of a body at the bottom of the stairs.
The plastic crinkling in darkness.
The silence of earth closing over breath.
She poured it into the room like ash into water,
a heavy, invisible tide.
Miriam's fingers twitched.
Her breath caught.
Her brow furrowed.
Somewhere in her sleep,
she turned her head toward the wall and whispered a name—
soft, broken.
"Lauren..."
But Harlan—
he smiled.
Still asleep.
Still dreaming.
Not at her.
Through her.
As if she were only fog on a window.
A passing cold front.

A nuisance to be outlasted.

He exhaled,

and the breath that passed from his mouth was not breath at all.

It was rot.

The scent of earth and plastic.

The scent of forgetting.

The demon hovered above him,

watching through the thin mask of flesh.

Unaffected.

Untouched.

Temperance recoiled slightly.

The pulse of the room warped around her.

She could not enter him.

Not yet.

He was sealed—

bound in flesh and denial,

the hunger coiled inside him like a second spine.

She looked down at Miriam.

Soft.

Fragile.

Still reachable.

But not tonight.

Not yet.

Temperance turned toward the hallway.

The house shifted around her like an animal sensing a change in the weather.

The hallway mirror still hung in its crooked way, just outside the younger girl's room.

For months it had gone quiet—just glass, just wood, just weight.

But now it pulsed faintly around the edges, as if the mahogany frame held more than polish and dust.

Temperance had moved through it once. She would again.

Not as shadow.

Not as curse.

But as rite.

As opening.

The hallway light flickered in nervous spasms.

A pulse.

A voice unspoken.

Temperance reached toward it.

Her fingers brushed the doorframe—

an almost-touch.

Then stopped.

She was not ready.

The blood was not ready.

Not yet.

But she would return.

Each night.

Until the Demon slipped.

Until the walls of silence crumbled.

Until the blood remembered what the mind refused.

And next time—

she would not whisper.

She would scream.

She would burn through the house like a second wind.

A tide that could not be turned back.

The girl stirred beneath the covers.

The house breathed.

And outside, beyond the reach of the porch light,

the trees bowed against a wind that had not yet arrived.

CHAPTER 22

THE UNRAVELING

Hamilton, Michigan – Spring 1991

Harlan had begun to misplace things.

His wrench.

His keys.

The second half of conversations.

He would walk into a room,

stand motionless,

brows knitting into confusion—

then turn around and return to the garage,

forgetting he had ever meant to do anything at all.

Miriam said nothing.

She watched from the doorway sometimes,

dishrag still in hand,

while he drifted through the kitchen like a ship unmoored.

He spent more time outside now.

Digging holes he never filled.

Piling tools in careful rows only to scatter them again the next day.

Checking the shed locks twice—

sometimes three times—
before wandering back inside.
The grass behind the garage grew taller than the rest.
A patchwork of untended green, leaning wild.
He did not cut it.
He told himself there were roots beneath the soil
that needed to stay untouched.
Some old agreement he could not break.
Some bargain too fragile to name.
Sometimes, he woke in the middle of the night.
Sat upright, breathing hard.
Listening.
He thought he heard someone knocking.
Three soft raps against the wall.
Then silence.
Always silence.
He blamed the plumbing.
Blamed the wind.
Blamed the newness of the house.
But the pipes were new.
The windows sealed.
The air still.
The knocks came anyway.
Soft.
Patient.
Counting him down.
He began to forget Miriam's birthday.
At first, he claimed he hadn't.
Then he insisted she had never told him.
And then—
as if rewriting the truth itself—
he said she never had one.

Miriam did not correct him.

She folded laundry.

Swept the kitchen.

Smiled when necessary.

The rooms grew colder.

The silences longer.

The mirrors began to warp.

At first, just the old ones.

The ones with tarnished backs and wavy glass.

But soon—

even the bathroom mirror, brand new,

twisted his reflection.

He caught glimpses of things—

his own face, but wrong.

Longer.

Thinner.

Empty around the eyes.

Sometimes, the face in the mirror smiled without him.

The heirloom mirror hung where they'd placed it weeks earlier—on the landing outside the bedroom, between the linen closet and the bedroom door. Heavy mahogany. The gilded phoenix tarnished to a whisper of gold. It had always felt too heavy for the drywall, but it had held.

Tonight, Harlan paused in front of it.

His reflection looked wrong.

The face that stared back was longer, thinner. Empty around the eyes. The mouth curled in a grin he hadn't formed.

Then—

it winked.

A slow, knowing blink.

He struck without thinking.

Fist to glass.

The impact echoed down the hall like a gunshot. The mirror

shuddered in its frame but did not fall. The glass spiderwebbed from the point of impact—radiating outward like frost on a windowpane.

Blood slid down the fractured surface in thin, elegant rivulets.

For a moment, it looked like the mirror was weeping.

Behind the cracks, his reflection blurred—

not gone, but fragmented.

Watching.

And just behind it—

something else moved.

Not him.

Not the woman.

Not quite either.

He stepped back, cradling his hand.

"Damn thing," he said, loud enough to be heard by no one.

Miriam found the blood later.

It had splashed high—higher than his shoulder.

A single arc of red kissed the ceiling corner.

She said nothing.

She fetched a rag.

Cleaned the floor.

Did not touch the mirror.

Temperance did not experience time as they did. Grief had no calendar. Rage had no clock.

The moment fractured her – not through glass, but across time. What he shattered in 1991 would not fully arrive until much later, in a woman's office lit by the quiet blue light of a computer screen.

That night, she dreamed of water running upward,

of glass sighing under breathless pressure,

of a woman's hair suspended in still air—

watching.

When she woke, the cracks in the mirror had vanished.

But something in it had changed.

The phoenix, now seemed to position its head, staring straight forward.

* * *

The younger daughter stopped going into the basement.
"It smells like dirt," she whispered once to Miriam.
"But not the good kind."
Miriam nodded.
She understood.
The earth had changed.
It whispered now beneath the floorboards.
A language too old to be translated.
Harlan started locking the garage at night.
Looping the padlock through the handle,
double-checking it with shaking hands.
But every morning—
the lock hung open.
Swaying lightly on its hinge.
Mocking him.
He stopped sleeping.
Started watching the trees.
He would sit in the kitchen for hours,
hands idle,
eyes fixed on the line where the backyard blurred into the woods.
Waiting.
For what, he didn't know.
But the trees knew.
They shifted when he wasn't looking.
Leaned closer.
Breathed.
And always—

just beyond the edges of his vision—
a woman stood.
Watching him back.
Hair like drifting smoke.
Eyes like winter storms.
Her body did not move.
She simply existed.
A fact.
A consequence.
She said nothing.
But her silence grew teeth.
Each night it pressed closer,
gnawed deeper,
worried at the edges of his mind.
And the thing inside him—
the thing sealed under skin and hunger—
began to stir again.
Not the hunger.
Not yet.
The fear.
Fear remembered the crack of bone.
The soft snap of a neck against the wall.
The slick sound of fabric tearing under cold hands.
Fear remembered what the mind refused to name.
Fear knew the blood had never cooled completely.
Fear whispered:
It is not finished.
Harlan paced the garage now like an animal trapped inside a shrinking
cage.
The air smelled wrong.
The walls leaned inward.
The ground outside pulsed when he tried to sleep.

The woman—
the smoke-haired watcher—
waited beyond the tree line.
Closer each night.
Her silence wove itself into his dreams.
And still he could not say her name.
Still he pretended he had forgotten.
But the soul does not forget.
The soil does not forget.
And the hunger inside him—
the thing stitched into his bones—
was beginning to remember.

CHAPTER 23:
THE LISTING

Florida – Winter 2010

Kathy stared at the screen like it might blink first.

The room was dark.

The only light came from the monitor,

casting long, pale shadows across the cluttered desk,

the stack of unopened letters,

the cold, untouched coffee sitting by her elbow.

The cursor blinked—

patient, rhythmic—

as though it already knew what she would find.

As though it had been waiting for her to finally ask.

She had typed the name five times.

Elara Badger.

Elara Badger.

Elara Badger.

Each time—

nothing.

The absence was worse than denial.

It was as if the world had swallowed her daughter whole.

Had never let her exist.
On a whim, hands trembling slightly,
Kathy typed the name she had seen once years ago—
buried deep in the thick packet of adoption paperwork
she had never fully been allowed to claim.
    Rockweiller.
The page loaded.
A face.
Familiar.
Not familiar in the way you recognize someone in a crowd.
Not familiar like an old friend.
No.
Familiar the way you know your own skin.
Your own breath.
The lines of her cheeks.
The shape of her eyes.
The curve of her mouth—
half-forgotten but never unloved.
It was her.
Her baby.
Grown.
Changed.
But her.
The photo was old.
A teenager.
The caption read:

    Missing.
    Since 1989.
    Last seen in West Michigan.

Kathy felt a chill bloom across her shoulders.

Not panic.

Not pain.

Something deeper.

The strange calm that comes

when the world finally admits

the thing your heart had whispered all along.

She clicked the image.

Watched it expand on the screen, pixel by pixel.

Read the details.

Height.

Age.

Last known location.

Each word a slow carving into her chest.

Michigan.

She whispered it aloud.

The sound of it cracked in her throat.

As if saying it would shatter the room.

The screen seemed to pulse.

The photo stared back.

Steady.

Waiting.

Behind her, the air shifted.

Softly.

Subtly.

She turned.

No one stood there.

But something had arrived.

Not presence.

Not yet.

A breath against the curtain.

A pressure in the walls.

A silence heavy enough to be named.

She turned back to the screen.
Opened her email tab.
The address felt strange under her fingers—
too official,
too sharp,
too full of consequence.

Her fingers hovered over the keys.
Then—
slowly, carefully—
she began to type.

"I believe I am the biological mother of the girl listed here.
Her name was Elara when I held her.
I know this is her.
I can offer DNA.
Please tell me someone is still looking for her."

The words trembled slightly on the screen.
Not from uncertainty.
From too much knowing.
In the hallway mirror outside her office,
the glass held steady—
but only just.
For days, Kathy had ignored its strange behavior.
A warping at the edges.
A faint shimmer like heat rising off asphalt.
She'd wiped it twice,
thinking it was residue.

But now—
now the surface pulsed.
Not violently.
Just… alive.
As though it recognized the name on the screen.
She stood.
Faced it.
The mirror offered her no distortion this time.
Only her own reflection—
and within it,

Temperance.

Not flickering.
Not fading.
Present.
Not a ghost.
Not a shadow.
A presence.
Kathy stepped forward, one hand half-lifted.
Then stopped.
The mirror cracked—
same spiderweb pattern,
same aching symmetry
as the mahogany mirror in Michigan
shattered beneath Harlan's fist
nineteen years earlier.
A mirror answering a mirror.
A wound remembered.
Her fingers trembled.
Not from fear.
From recognition.

Somewhere in the mirror, something recalled her.

Her blood.

Her grief.

Her vow.

She turned back to the screen.

Her voice did not shake as she whispered.

"Now."

She signed her name carefully.

Kathy Badger.

She clicked Send.

A pale figure stood in the mirror.

Hair floating as if underwater.

Eyes wide with gathering storm.

Temperance.

No longer only smoke.

No longer only memory.

Awake.

Fully.

Present.

She turned slowly—

toward Kathy.

Toward the screen.

Toward the future that had refused to die.

The email sent with a soft chime.

The screen blinked.

Outside, a wind rose against the side of the house—

a wind that had not been forecasted.

The curtains lifted as if breathing.

The house listened.

The ground remembered.

And somewhere,
across state lines and bone-deep silences,
something shifted in the roots.
The tether pulled tight again.
Not undone.
Not broken.
Straining toward reckoning.
Temperance did not fade.
She did not vanish.
She stood vigil in the glass,
her reflection no longer waiting.
She was not alone anymore.
Not in memory.
Not in grief.
Not in rage.
The house shivered around her.
And in the unseen corners of the world—
the dark places where truth had been buried too long—
the blood began to stir.

CHAPTER 24:
THE REQUEST

Hamilton, Michigan – Spring 2010

The envelope arrived on a Wednesday.

Plain.

Official.

No fanfare, no urgency.

It was tucked between a grocery flyer and a charity appeal, folded tight in the metal mouth of the mailbox as if trying to hide.

Miriam plucked it free without thinking.

She carried it inside alongside a bag of onions and a bottle of dish soap.

Set it down beside the sink.

Forgot it there while folding towels.

It wasn't until the light began to shift—

that long, golden slope of late afternoon—

that she noticed it again.

Her hands dry from laundry,

she picked it up.

Turned it over.

Her name.

Her address.
The return corner read:

Michigan State Police – Cold Case Division

She paused.
The kitchen was too quiet.
The faucet dripped once.
The clock ticked louder than it should have.
The walls seemed to lean closer, listening.
Quietly, Miriam opened it.
The paper was thin, institutional.
The letter was short.
Formal.
A reopened investigation, it said.

Regarding the 1989 disappearance of her daughter, Lauren Rockweiller.

They were requesting updated DNA samples—
to assist in confirming or ruling out matches in the national database.
Routine.
Procedural.
Polite.
Miriam read it once.
Then again.
And again.
The words did not change.
But something inside her did.
Not grief.
Not fear.
Something older.
Something like breath turning inward,

folding itself small enough to survive.

She looked toward the garage.

Harlan was in there—

where he always was when the weather warmed.

Tinkering.

Sweeping.

Fixing things that didn't need fixing.

The door hung half open.

Light poured across the concrete floor,

catching along the curve of a familiar barrel tucked in the shadow.

The same blue.

The same silence.

Miriam folded the letter.

Slid it into the back of her Bible.

The one she kept in the drawer beneath the telephone.

The one with the cracked spine,

the ribbon still caught between Psalms and prophecy.

She said nothing to Harlan.

Not that day.

Not that night.

That evening, the mirrors grew louder.

They did not speak—

not in words.

But they hummed.

A low vibration,

like a mouth pressed against glass.

Like breath trapped in a jar too long.

The hallway mirror trembled faintly.

The bathroom mirror misted at the edges,

though no water had been run.

Miriam moved carefully through the house.

Turned off every light.

Closed the curtains.
Tucked the younger daughter into bed,
brushing her hair with slow, reverent strokes.
Longer than necessary.
Longer than comfort required.
She kissed the girl's forehead.
Listened to her breathing settle.
Then Miriam went to her own room.
Lay down beside Harlan.
His breath was even.
Slow.
He smelled of soil and oil and sweat—
the trinity of his forgetting.
He did not stir.
He never did anymore.
Miriam stared at the ceiling.
Above them, the house held its breath.
Below them,
the earth behind the garage—
the loosened earth—
felt somehow warm.
As if something beneath it had started to stir.
As if memory could rise like heat through soil.
The letter remained tucked between pages.
Waiting.
Patient.
It did not demand.
It did not accuse.
It simply existed.
Proof pressed between prophecy and prayer.
Outside, beyond the fence,
beyond the last line of trimmed grass,

Temperance stood among the pines.

No longer distant.

No longer spectral.

Fully awake.

Her hair floated behind her as if suspended in water.

Her eyes were wide and unblinking.

She was not watching the house in mourning now.

She was watching it in certainty.

She had not come to warn.

She had come to remember.

And to make others remember.

The wind pressed against the windowpane once.

Not with violence.

With intent.

The swing set moved.

Once.

Then still.

Miriam closed her eyes.

But she did not sleep.

Not for a long time.

The ceiling held her gaze.

The letter pressed into the Bible waited.

The house exhaled slowly—like something trying to be patient.

The soil behind the garage breathed in.

Temperance stood.

Unmoving.

Her presence folded into the roots,

into the walls,

into the places where truth had been buried too long.

She did not move closer yet.

She did not knock yet.

But she would.

Very soon.
Because the blood was stirring.
The bones were listening.
And this time—
the dead would not be forgotten.

CHAPTER 25:
THE FIRST BREAK

Hamilton, Michigan – Summer 2010

The mirror in the hallway shattered at 2:13 a.m.

There was no storm.

No quake.

No footsteps on the stairs.

Just the sound—

a clean, sharp crack—

like a bone snapping in reverse.

A sound that broke the air without raising its voice.

Miriam woke first.

She didn't move.

Didn't gasp.

Didn't reach for Harlan or the lamp.

She simply opened her eyes

and stared into the dark.

The air felt wrong.

Heavy.

Tight.

Like the whole house had exhaled once
and forgotten how to breathe back in.
Beside her, Harlan shifted—
mumbling through a dream he would not remember.
His breathing stayed thick and steady,
drenched in sweat.
The fan at the foot of the bed hummed on,
oblivious.
Outside, the trees did not stir.
The world had gone still,
but not silent.
The stillness buzzed.
A hum beneath hearing.
A low, living tremor.
Miriam rose.
Her bare feet found the floor,
the boards colder than they should have been.
The hallway was dim,
lit only by the faint, stubborn glow of the bathroom nightlight.
She moved toward the sound.
Glass everywhere.
It glittered across the carpet
like frost under moonlight.
The mirror's frame still hung stubbornly on the wall—
empty.
Its silver backing was gone,
ripped like skin torn from flesh.
Inside, where she should have seen wall studs and plaster,
there was only black.
Not void.
Absence.
A depth that drank the light.

A wound that refused to heal.

Miriam stood,

barefoot on the threshold of it.

She didn't step closer.

She didn't turn away.

She just listened.

The air around her vibrated.

A hum.

Low and distant.

Alive.

Like something breathing against glass from the other side.

Then it came.

A whisper.

Not sound.

Meaning.

Not a voice she could hear.

But a presence she could not deny.

It's not enough to be seen.

Miriam's breath caught.

Something pressed against the inside of her skin—

a memory she didn't know she had.

A shiver along the ribs.

A crack opening somewhere deep within.

She backed away slowly.

Controlled.

Her heel found a shard of glass.

She felt the bite,

the wet bloom of blood across her foot.

But she did not flinch.

Did not feel the pain.

Behind her, the bedroom door creaked open.

But no one stood there.

Only the empty frame,
gaping like a mouth about to speak.
She turned.
The mirror's frame was now—
empty.
Not broken.
Not jagged.
Just—
absent.
As if it had never held glass at all.
The broken pieces were gone.
Cleaned.
Erased.
Swallowed.
But the wall behind it remained wrong.
Too deep.
Too still.
As if the house had decided to remember something—
and could no longer bear to hold it in.
Miriam reached for the light switch.
It flickered once.
A quick gasp of electricity.
Then steadied.
She caught the movement from the corner of her eye.
A face.
In the glass of the hallway cabinet—briefly—
a reflection that was not her own.
Not Harlan's.
A woman.
Hair like driftwood—
darkened by unseen currents.
Eyes like stormlight—

wide and breaking.

Temperance.
She stood just beyond the reflection.
Hand raised.
Palm pressed against the invisible barrier.
Her mouth did not move.
But the silence around her grew teeth.
The house seemed to tilt slightly.
The air tightened—
a drumhead stretched too far.
Miriam turned.
The image vanished.
But she knew.
She had always known.
She walked back to the bedroom.
Her foot left small dots of blood along the carpet.
She did not wipe them away.
Did not hesitate.
She climbed beneath the covers beside Harlan.
He did not stir.
Did not wake.
The fan hummed on.
The world outside held its breath.
Miriam lay still.
Did not speak.
Did not cry.
She closed her eyes.
And in the black behind her lids—
the mirror broke again.
Only this time—
it didn't shatter.

It opened.
A wound.
A door.
A memory.
Something old and holy
torn wide in the skin of the house.
Something that would not heal.
Something that would not be silenced again.

CHAPTER 26

THE ARREST

Hamilton, Michigan – November 2019

It began with the knock.

Not loud.

Not urgent.

Just three steady taps at the door,

like the house itself had exhaled,

and could no longer hold the weight of what it knew.

Harlan stood in the kitchen, pouring coffee.

Miriam was folding laundry,

moving slowly, methodically—

like the rhythm itself could keep the world from fraying apart.

The younger daughter was long grown and gone.

The house was quieter than ever.

Quieter than it should have been.

The knock came again.

Steady.

Measuring.

Harlan wiped his hands on a dishtowel.

Walked to the front door.

Opened it.

Two officers.

Badges visible.

Voices calm.

Neutral.

Practiced.

A name spoken.

"Harlan Rockweiller?"

"Yes."

Another name spoken.

A colder one.

"You're under arrest for the murder of Celeste Morrel."

Miriam dropped the towel she was folding.

It fell to the floor like a fallen bird.

A name—

Celeste Morrel.

One she hadn't heard in decades.

One she had almost—

but not quite—

forgotten.

A murder in Norfolk, Virginia.

A wound she had never seen stitched.

Only buried.

Deep.

Harlan didn't move.

Not at first.

He stared past the officers,

past the porch,

past the street—

into the line of trees at the edge of the yard.

As if expecting to see her there.

Temperance.

But the yard was empty.

Only the battered outline of where the swing used to be.

Only the weight of a memory that refused to be banished.

The officers shifted.

One reached for cuffs.

Still, Harlan did not resist.

He set the coffee mug gently into the sink.

Held out his hands.

The metal of the cuffs clicked into place.

A sound too small to carry the gravity of the moment.

But it did.

It did.

They led him down the porch steps.

The air was cold.

November's breath was sharp against the skin.

The sky hung low and dull,

a sheet of pewter stretched across the bones of the world.

Neighbors watched from behind thin curtains.

Faces pressed close to the glass.

Miriam stood in the doorway,

hands limp at her sides.

She said nothing.

She did not call out.

Did not ask why.

She already knew.

She had always known.

Harlan didn't look back.

Not once.

But as he stepped off the final stair,

he stumbled.

His foot caught on nothing.

Gravity took him.
He dropped to one knee.
A breath escaped him—
sharp, wounded.
And when he lifted his head—
he saw her.
Beneath the oldest tree at the edge of the yard,
where the grass grew uneven and wild,
stood Temperance.
Pale.
Unblinking.
Her hair moved as if underwater,
touched by a current the living could not feel.
Her eyes fixed on him.
Wide.
Immovable.
She said nothing.
She did not need to.
Her presence pressed against him
like a second gravity.
The weight of memory.
The weight of blood.
The weight of promises broken beyond mending.
Inside him,
the demon stirred.
Not with hunger.
Not with rage.
With recognition.
And retreat.
A shrinking backward.
A folding in on itself.
It had faced many things.

But it had never faced being remembered.

Not fully.

Not with eyes like hers.

The officers lifted Harlan to his feet.

One read him his rights.

The words floated through the air,

thin and brittle as autumn leaves.

The other opened the cruiser door.

The world narrowed.

Closed.

Tightened.

Behind him, the house stood silent.

Watching.

Waiting.

Remembering.

Beneath the soil of the backyard,

deep under the tangled roots of long-forgotten trees,

the ground groaned.

A low, shuddering exhale.

A sound of earth remembering what had been buried.

The reckoning had arrived.

Not with sirens.

Not with fire.

But with a silence too loud to ignore.

Temperance remained hovering within the tree.

Her body still.

Her hair drifting.

Her eyes wide and merciless.

Not as a spirit.

Not as a ghost.

But as a reckoning given form.

Harlan ducked into the cruiser.

The door closed.
Metal on metal.
A seal.
A tomb.
The car pulled away from the curb.
Miriam stood at the doorway,
the cold air gathering around her feet.
She did not step outside.
She did not wave.
She simply watched him leave.
And for the first time in years—
the house behind her exhaled.
Not in relief.
In mourning.
Temperance turned from the yard.
Whispered back into the line of trees.
And was gone.
But her shadow lingered.
Woven now into the grain of the house,
the bones of the yard,
the breath of the soil.
There are reckonings that shout.
And there are reckonings that wait.
This was the second kind.
The one that never ends.

C H A P T E R 2 7:
THE WALK

Hamilton, Michigan – Days After the Arrest

The house was still.

Not empty.

Still.

The kind of stillness that settles after a scream has gone hoarse.

The kind that comes when something too heavy to move finally gives up.

Miriam stood at the back door.

Her coat in one hand.

She hadn't gone outside in three days.

Reporters had come and gone,

leaving behind smudges of breath on the windows.

Neighbors whispered from behind fences—

voices thin and curling like smoke.

Phones rang.

And rang.

And rang.

She let them.

They didn't matter now.
Nothing urgent remained.
Only this.
Only the silence waiting.
She stepped outside.
Into the cold.
The air tasted of rust and brittle leaves.
The grass was sharp against her ankles—
crisp with frost,
breaking underfoot like old paper.
The wind moved across her skin not like air—
but like water.
Dense.
Pressing.
Carrying old names.
The garden was long dead.
Overgrown with weeds that wound through the soil like veins.
The swing set stood rusted and hollow.
A rib cage with no breath left in it.
Bones clinging to memory.
Miriam followed the path behind the garage—
past the shed,
past the line where the mown lawn gave way to wildness.
To the shovel.
Still there.
Leaning against the fence.
Its handle splintered.
Its blade rusted through.
Half-buried now in a clot of stubborn mud.
The earth around it was wrong.
Uneven.
Sunken slightly.

The kind of sinking that doesn't come from rain alone.

The kind that remembers.

She crouched.

Knees cracking softly in the cold.

Pressed her palm to the ground.

It was warm.

Too warm for November.

The warmth of something living.

Or something refusing to be forgotten.

She sat fully.

Folded her legs beneath her.

Coat pooling like a second skin.

Pressed her hand flat again to the dirt.

Closed her eyes.

Breathed.

Listened.

The wind stopped.

As if the world were holding its breath for her.

The silence thickened.

It wasn't empty.

It was pregnant.

Waiting.

And for the first time in years,

Miriam whispered the name.

The true one.

The first one.

The only one that mattered.

"Lauren."

The ground did not shift.

The trees did not bow.

The sky did not crack open.

But something passed through her chest—

a pressure.
Ancient.
Immense.
Not violence.
Not grace.
A grief too large to belong to one woman alone.
A sorrow that had waited too long to be named.
It moved through her like a tide without water—
hollowing her,
filling her.
Behind her, the swing moved.
Just once.
A slow, sighing arc.
Then stillness.
Not reset.
Not erased.
Consecrated.
Miriam did not cry.
Did not scream.
She simply stayed there,
hand to the earth,
breath shallow but steady.
Listening.
Waiting.
And from somewhere just beyond the pines—
half-shadow,
half-memory—
a woman stood.
Temperance.
Not draped in rage.
Not burdened by wrath.
She stood quietly.

Still as a prayer.

Her hair floated behind her like riverweed caught in a current too slow to see.

Her eyes were wide.

Full.

Heavy with memory.

But there was no judgment there.

No fury.

Only something quieter.

Sadder.

Older.

Recognition.

And perhaps—

just perhaps—

forgiveness.

Miriam opened her eyes.

She did not rise.

Did not turn.

She didn't need to.

She knew.

The soil knew.

The blood knew.

The house knew.

She pressed her hand deeper into the earth.

Felt the slow pulse of something ancient stir beneath her palm.

A heartbeat not her own.

A memory refusing to die quietly.

The wind picked up again—

whispering through the trees.

But it did not chill her.

It cradled her.

A slow, solemn embrace.

A promise written in breath.
And for the first time in her long, fractured life—
Miriam did not fear remembering.
She did not fear the sound of her own grief rising.
She was part of it now.
Threaded through.
Named and naming.
Remembered.
The earth sighed.
The house listened.
And beyond the fence,
Temperance turned toward the deeper woods.
Her figure thinning into mist.
Not vanishing.
Not erased.
Folded into the weave of the living world.
Waiting for what must come next.

CHAPTER 28

THE INTERVIEW

County Jail, Michigan – December 2019

The interview room was bare.

No windows.

One table.

Two chairs.

A fan in the ceiling turned with mechanical indifference,

its slow, uneven rotation clicking faintly every fourth pass.

The fluorescent light buzzed overhead—

an impatient noise against the hush of the concrete walls.

Harlan sat still.

Wrists cuffed to the loop bolted into the center of the table.

The collar of his orange jumpsuit sat uneven on his neck—

as if it had been yanked too hard in one direction

and never forgiven.

He hadn't asked for a lawyer.

Hadn't spoken since booking.

Had only accepted the coffee they offered him—

black, lukewarm, inert.

He drank it slowly.

Quietly.

Watching the steam rise from the cup,

as if the air itself might carry messages only he could decode.

Detective Alan Riddick sat across from him.

Mid-fifties.

Methodical.

Worn, but not soft.

The kind of man who spoke in single sentences

and let silence do the heavy lifting.

His folder remained closed.

His pen was capped.

The recorder blinked red in the center of the table.

Patient.

Waiting.

Harlan's gaze shifted lazily toward it.

Then toward Riddick.

"It doesn't like to be recorded," Harlan said.

His voice was flat.

Almost conversational.

Riddick raised an eyebrow.

"What doesn't?"

Harlan smiled faintly.

Not pleased.

Just present.

"The thing that comes through," he said.

"The other part."

Riddick didn't write it down.

Didn't blink.

Only nodded slightly—

as if to say: Go on.

"You understand you've been charged," Riddick said,

"with the murder of Celeste Morrel."

Harlan looked down at his hands,

turning them slightly as if seeing them for the first time.

The cuffs rattled softly.

"You didn't ask me if I did it," he said.

"I didn't need to."

Silence filled the room.

Thick.

Settled.

Alive.

The fan turned overhead,

straining against its own rhythm.

Riddick leaned forward slightly.

Not aggressive.

Just closer.

"Tell me about Norfolk," he said.

"Tell me where you were in 1980."

Harlan's mouth twitched.

Something between a grimace and a memory.

"I was with my wife," he said.

"In Michigan."

Riddick nodded once.

Flat.

Patient.

"She says the same."

"Then you have your answer."

"But you weren't," Riddick said.

Quietly.

Without inflection.

Harlan said nothing.

The stillness of him sharpened.

A coiled thing.

A house that had locked its doors too late.

Riddick opened the file slowly—

a whisper of paper against paper.

Photographs slid free.

Black-and-white.

Crime scene images.

Celeste's small house.

The broken lamp.

The overturned mattress.

The trail of bruises.

And finally—

the girl herself.

Her hair spread like kelp across the still white stained mattress.

Eyes open.

Mouth slack.

"She tried to fight back," Riddick said.

His voice was almost tender.

"The coroner said there was a serious struggle."

"Someone disconnected the phone. Sounds pre-meditated."

Harlan stared at the images without blinking.

His pupils contracted slightly under the flicker of the fluorescent light.

He said nothing.

Riddick waited.

Two seconds.

Three.

Four.

Patience weaponized.

Finally, Harlan spoke.

But not to the detective.

Not really.

"She reminded it of something," he said softly.

"What did she remind you of?" Riddick asked.

Harlan smiled again.

A hollow, broken thing.

"Not me," he whispered.

"The other part."

The fan creaked once overhead.

The lights buzzed.

The coffee cooled between them.

Riddick leaned back.

Studied him.

Said nothing.

The demon stirred beneath Harlan's skin.

Not roaring.

Not lashing.

Just—

moving.

A tremor behind the ribs.

A whisper behind the teeth.

A memory without permission.

"You know," Harlan said, his voice almost kind,

"they always think it's rage."

He tilted his head slightly—

like a man explaining a simple truth to a child.

"But it's not."

"What is it then?" Riddick asked.

Harlan smiled wider.

Closed his eyes.

Silence again.

Deeper this time.

The kind that thins the air.

The kind that lets old things breathe.

The recorder blinked red.

Recording every word.

Every absence.

Every breath.

Riddick closed the file.

Snapped the pen cap into place.

Gathered the photographs slowly, methodically.

Tucked them back without hurry.

Harlan sat motionless.

His hands flat against the table now—

as if anchoring himself to it.

Or waiting for it to anchor him.

"You'll be moved to holding tonight," Riddick said.

"We'll have more questions later."

Harlan nodded.

Almost absent-mindedly.

As if none of this had anything to do with him anymore.

As if he were only the last echo of something already faded.

As the detective rose,

the lights overhead flickered once.

Just once.

A soft, almost apologetic stutter.

Riddick paused at the door.

Turned back.

"One last thing," he said.

Harlan opened his eyes.

Met his gaze.

"Did you bury her?"

Harlan smiled.

This time—

with teeth.

He remained silent.

The fan turned.

The recorder blinked.

The air grew heavier.
And somewhere far beyond the jail walls,
beneath the frozen earth of a forgotten backyard—
the ground tightened its hold.
Waiting.
Listening.
Remembering.

CHAPTER 29:
THE DNA

County Jail, Michigan – January 2020

They had asked, once.

Years ago.

A polite letter, tucked between bills and coupons.

A request phrased like routine.

Like mercy.

Harlan and Miriam both responded.

They had mailed their vials.

Taped the seal.

Never mentioned it again.

And now—

now that the past had grown teeth—

Memory curled into the microscopes and science.

The DNA recovered from the stained mattress in Celeste Morrel's house—

matched the man now sitting in a Michigan jail cell.

There was no ambiguity.

No degraded sample.

No technician's hesitation.

No chain of custody doubt.

Clean.

Final.

He had been there.

He had touched her.

He had entered her.

And he had not left alone.

Detective Riddick read the results three times

before bringing them to the department.

Then once more, alone,

just to feel the weight of what they meant.

"Definitive," the report read.

"No exclusion."

When they told Harlan,

he said nothing.

He sat across from Riddick,

the paper laid between them like scripture.

The red light on the recorder blinked—

steady, small.

"You're not surprised," Riddick said.

"No," Harlan said.

His voice was dry.

Empty.

"You're not denying it anymore."

"I never denied what happened," Harlan said.

"Only who was awake when it did."

Silence stretched across the room.

The fan ticked.

A door slammed far down the corridor.

"You understand what this means," Riddick said.

"Yes."

"No more riddles," Riddick added.

A warning, not a plea.

Harlan looked up then.

Eyes clear.

Focused.

"I don't have riddles," he said.

"Only gaps."

"Gaps?" Riddick asked.

"In time.

In memory.

In mercy."

The air bent slightly.

The fluorescent lights hummed louder,

as if protesting the shape of the conversation.

"I remember watching it happen," Harlan said.

"But not from here."

He tapped his chest with two fingers.

Then gestured behind him.

"From there," he said.

"Like I was just... floating."

"Floating," Riddick repeated.

Dry. Skeptical.

"Just outside myself," Harlan whispered.

"You expect a jury to believe that?"

"I don't expect anything," Harlan said.

Riddick narrowed his eyes.

Voice sharpening.

"You think if you dress it in poetry,

we'll forget the blood?"

"No," Harlan said.

"I think if I tell the truth,

you'll call it madness."

The fan ticked overhead.

"Do you believe you killed her?" Riddick asked.

Harlan's jaw worked slightly—

as if chewing on something he couldn't swallow.

"I believe something in me did," he said.

"Something I can't name

without giving it too much power."

"You're not the first man to claim a monster," Riddick said.

"Most of them do it after they're caught."

Harlan looked at him.

And smiled.

But the smile didn't touch his eyes.

It hollowed them.

"It's not in me," he said.

"It is me."

For the first time,

Riddick felt the air change.

Not colder.

Not hotter.

Just—

wrong.

As if the atmosphere had tilted slightly sideways.

Harlan leaned forward.

The cuffs clinked.

"Would you like to know what it feels like?" he asked.

Riddick said nothing.

"It feels," Harlan said, voice low,

"like waking up with your hands covered in something warm—

and thinking, not again."

"It feels like watching your wife brush her hair

and wondering if she'll smell the rot on your skin."

"It feels like waiting for something to crawl out of you—

and realizing it already did."

His voice did not rise.

But it vibrated.

As if something ancient

had climbed into his vocal cords

and begun to strum them like strings.

Riddick closed the file.

Slowly.

Deliberately.

The red light on the recorder blinked one final time.

Then stopped.

He stood.

Gathered the folder under his arm.

"Thank you for your time, Mr. Rockweiller," he said.

Harlan leaned back in his chair.

Expression unreadable.

"You're welcome," he said.

"But I didn't give you time."

Riddick paused at the door.

Turned.

"What did you give me then?"

Harlan smiled again.

This time—emptier.

Colder.

A mirror without reflection.

"A warning," he said.

The door closed.

Soft.

Deliberate.

Inside the room, the air stilled.

The fan hesitated mid-turn.

The lights flickered once.

And in the mirror on the far wall—
for just a breath—
something leaned close.
The silvered surface warped.
Not cracked.
Not broken.
Just—
breathed.
As if something on the other side had pressed its face to the glass—
and whispered.

CHAPTER 30:
THE CALL

Hamilton, Michigan – January 2020

The phone rang at 3:41 p.m.

Miriam had just finished washing the teacup.

The sun slanted low through the kitchen window, striking the glass and turning the counter amber. The water in the sink was still warm, scented faintly with lavender and old porcelain.

She dried her hands slowly.

Did not hurry to answer.

When she finally picked up, the line was already breathing.

Not static.

Breath.

Then a voice.

Low. Familiar. Strained.

"Miriam?"

Her fingers curled around the receiver.

She said nothing.

"It's me," Harlan added, though he didn't need to.

The silence stretched.

Not cold.

Not forgiving.

Just... awake.

He cleared his throat.

"They let me make a call."

Still she didn't speak.

"I figured you'd want to hear it from me."

Pause.

"They're saying things, about Virginia. About that girl."

Another pause.

"You remember, right? I wasn't even there. That weekend, remember the snow? You made that chili I like. I helped with the pipes in the basement. That was—January? February?"

Her voice, when it came, was quiet.

Flat.

"You went to Norfolk."

The silence that followed wasn't surprise.

It was calculation.

Then: "No. That's not right. I told you about that trip. Later. Maybe years later. But not then."

She let the lie hang there.

Unanswered.

Unfed.

"They've got some kind of DNA thing," he added, voice sharpening.

"Said they matched me to something. A sheet or—something." He exhaled hard. "That's not proof. That's not—look, I never touched her."

Miriam's voice didn't rise.

"Detective Riddick came by."

That slowed him.

"What did he tell you?"

"He said the DNA was conclusive. No degradation. No doubt."

A long breath on the other end of the line.

And then—

"So what now?" Harlan asked.

It wasn't a question.

Not really.

A performance of one.

"You tell the truth," she said.

Her voice was clear now.

The kitchen light caught the window glass and reflected back the outline of her face, doubled and pale.

"You think I haven't been?" he asked, voice rising faintly.

"You haven't," she said.

Another pause.

"I didn't mean for any of it to happen," he said finally.

Miriam closed her eyes.

The silence became a kind of weight in her hand.

A cord stretched between them—fraying.

"Do you believe I can be forgiven?" he asked.

There it was.

The crack behind the voice.

The rust behind the breath.

She touched the wall with her free hand, palm flat against the plaster, as if listening for something deeper than words.

After a long time, she said:

"That's not mine to give."

He said her name again, but this time it didn't sound like a plea.

It sounded like a man trying to remember how it used to feel.

She hung up.

The line went dead with a soft click.

She did not cry.

She did not speak.

She stood there, listening to the quiet, as if the house had something left to say.

And in the hallway mirror—

the heirloom mirror with the gilded phoenix—

the silvered glass pulsed once.

Just once.

As if it had drawn breath.

Miriam turned toward it.

And saw her.

Temperance.

Not floating now.

Not translucent.

Still.

Present.

Her reflection layered faintly over Miriam's own—eyes aligned, mouth closed, breath shared.

She was not smiling.

But she was certain.

And in her certainty, there was power.

The power of persistence.

Of a mother's reach.

Of a woman's vow.

Temperance did not speak.

But Miriam understood.

Everything that was happening—this slow fracture, this gathering storm—had begun the moment Kathy typed that name.

Elara.

And Temperance had been there.

Carrying the letter.

Lighting the screen.

Turning the breath of grief into action.

Miriam touched the edge of the mirror.

Warm.

Alive.

A tether, not a trap.

A reckoning born from care.

And behind her reflection, Temperance held steady.

Not demanding justice.

Becoming it.

CHAPTER 31

THE CONFESSION

Muskegon County Jail – October 2020

The cell was silent.

The air thick with unspoken truths.

The kind of silence that knew what had been said before it was spoken.

Harlan sat at the metal table.

Hands clasped.

Eyes fixed on the scuffed surface.

Breath shallow.

Pulse steady.

As if bracing for something inevitable.

Detective Alan Riddick entered.

A folder tucked under his arm.

He crossed the room without hurry.

Pulled the opposite chair back with a soft scrape.

Sat down.

"Harlan," Riddick began.

His voice steady.

Measured.

"We've matched your DNA to evidence from the Celeste Morrel case."

He laid the folder flat.

Opened it.

Photographs.

Lab reports.

Printouts with dates and signatures.

"The DNA found on her mattress," Riddick continued,

"is your DNA."

Harlan's gaze didn't flicker.

Didn't twitch.

He stared down at his clasped hands.

Still.

"You've already been through that with me."

Waiting.

"But that's not the only reason I'm here," Riddick said.

His voice dipped lower.

Closer.

He leaned forward.

Elbows braced on the table.

"We know about Lauren."

Harlan didn't blink.

Didn't breathe any deeper.

But something beneath his skin shifted—

a crack along an old foundation.

A groan too deep to echo.

The detective pressed.

"We know she didn't run away."

Pause.

"We know she's still here."

Longer pause.

"Somewhere close."

A silence stretched.

Not absence.

Weight.

Waiting to break.

"She is," Harlan said.

His tone was flat.

Uninflected.

But something beneath it splintered.

Like a beam snapping under new weight.

Riddick reached into his coat.

Pulled out a second file.

Thinner.

Raw.

Unconfirmed.

"There are people looking now," Riddick said.

"Old neighbors. Witness statements."

He hesitated.

Measured the next name carefully.

"A woman came forward last month."

"Kathy Badger."

Still, Harlan didn't move.

Didn't blink.

Didn't breathe.

"Says she's the biological mother," Riddick said.

"Says she knows where Lauren is."

Harlan's jaw tightened.

Just once.

Small.

Sharp.

"She says she saw her," Riddick added.

"Or... felt her."

Pause.

"Buried somewhere near your garage.

In your backyard."

The silence that followed was not empty.

It was thick.

A black tide pressing at the seams of the room.

Harlan's eyes flicked to the images on the table.

Then back to the scuffed metal surface.

"You want to talk about Lauren," he said.

"Yes," Riddick said.

"It's time we discuss what happened to her."

Harlan sighed.

The weight of decades exhaling through his ribs.

"She was..." he began.

He faltered.

Started again.

"She was trying to leave."

Pause.

"Said she'd tell someone."

Pause.

"Tell someone about what I'd done."

Riddick's voice stayed calm.

Steady.

"What did you do, Harlan?"

The detective rose slightly from his chair.

Not walking away.

Just standing.

Letting the silence flood the space between them.

Harlan hesitated.

Then—

barely above a whisper:

"I slapped her."

Silence.

"She fell down the stairs."

Silence heavier now.

Filling the gaps between each word like concrete.

"It was an accident."

Riddick leaned forward.

Closer.

"And then?"

Harlan closed his eyes.

A tremor moved through him—

barely perceptible.

"I panicked," he whispered.

"I didn't know what to do."

Pause.

"I... I buried her."

The air shifted.

Tightened.

The fan overhead ticked once.

"There's more, isn't there?" Riddick asked.

Harlan opened his eyes.

Haunted now.

Hollow.

Heavy with something older than guilt.

"There's something inside me," Harlan said.

"A darkness."

Pause.

"It takes over."

He tapped the table once with his fingers.

A soft, hollow sound.

"I need paper," he said.

"And something to draw with."

Detective Riddick hesitated.

Then nodded.

Signaled through the window.

A guard brought a yellow legal pad.

A dull pencil.

Harlan pulled the pad close.

Placed his palm flat against the paper.

Closed his eyes.

Breathed once.

Then began.

He drew a circle.

Small.

Perfect.

Black.

No shading.

No frills.

Just absence.

"It starts here," Harlan said.

Tapping the center with the pencil.

"Right in the chest."

"Beneath the bone."

"Behind the breath."

His voice shifted.

Not louder.

Deeper.

Older.

As if something else had slipped through his vocal cords

and begun to speak.

"It begins as a wound," he said.

"A hollow."

"You don't notice it at first."

"It's cold—

but not painful."

"It waits."

He drew another ring.

Wider now.

The paper darkening.

The circle swelling outward.

"And then it opens."

A third ring.

Heavy now.

The page trembling slightly under the pressure of his hand.

"It doesn't come from outside," he whispered.

"It unfolds."

"From within."

"Like remembering something you never knew you forgot."

He pressed harder.

The lead cracked slightly under his grip.

"And when the circle is wide enough—"

Pause.

"When the ribs forget their shape—"

Pause.

"Then it comes."

He drew a little devil.

Two horns.

Riddick said nothing.

Only watched.

Harlan raised his head slowly.

His pupils wide.

Blown open.

His voice no longer entirely his own.

"The demon is not possession," he said.

"It is permission."

"I don't watch it."

He leaned closer.

Cuffs rattling.

"I am it."

Pause.

"But only in the moment it breathes through me."

Pause.

"And then it retracts—

leaves me coated in what it did."

"What I did."

"I don't know the difference anymore."

He slid the page forward.

Riddick looked down.

The circle wasn't just black.

It was deep.

A hollow burned into the paper.

A shape stared back from the center—

not an eye.

Not a face.

A pressure.

A pull.

A hole in the world.

"This," Harlan said,

his voice thin and ragged now,

"is what took Lauren."

And somewhere—

far below the concrete of the jail,

beneath the layers of buried years—

the hunger exhaled.

Riddick studied the image.

Felt the wrongness vibrating off the page.

Ominous.

Foreboding.

Alive.

"Thank you for sharing this," Riddick said finally.

Voice even.

But his hand trembled slightly as he gathered the materials.

He stood.

Harlan remained seated.

Motionless.

The weight of his confession settling over him like dust.

Like ash.

In the quiet that followed,

Harlan whispered:

"Elara."

Soft.

Fractured.

Sacred.

And from the depths of his being,

the darkness stirred once more.

Not roaring.

Not claiming.

Just—

waiting..

CHAPTER 32:
ANOTHER CALL

Hamilton, Michigan – November 2020

The letters had been strange at first.
Stiff.
Measured.
Too formal by half.
But over time, they softened.
Handwritten in neat, careful loops—
the way he used to write notes to her
on folded napkins at the diner,
before she knew what silence could cost.
They came every few weeks now.
Thin envelopes,
carrying the weight of a man trying to hold onto something
that still made him human.
She kept them in a shoebox under her bed.
Tied with ribbon.
Not out of sentiment.
Out of habit.

Out of hope.
She read them at night,
when the wind was high
and the mirrors too quiet.
When memory crowded her shoulders,
but grief refused to speak its name.
The phone rang just past 6 p.m.
The light was low in the kitchen.
Golden across the linoleum.
A roast in the oven.
Her hands damp from rinsing carrots.
She let it ring once.
Twice.
Then picked up.
"Hello?"
A pause.
Then—
"Miriam."
His voice.
familiar.
Gentle.
Somehow still carrying the cadence of the man
who once drove her to Lake Michigan in a borrowed truck
and kissed her beneath a gull-choked sky.
"Harlan."
She said it like a blessing.
Or a wound reopened without complaint.
"I didn't know if you'd answer."
"I always answer," she said.
Another pause.
Not tense.
Just full.

He cleared his throat.

"How's the roast?"

She smiled, in spite of herself.

"It's fine. A little dry."

"You always overcook it."

"You always said that."

Silence again.

But softer now.

A silence made of long roads

and longer forgiveness. "No."

A breath.

"I've been thinking," Harlan said.

"About you. About us."

Miriam sat down at the kitchen table.

The chair creaked beneath her.

The kitchen ticked with small domestic sounds—

the timer on the oven,

the drip of the faucet.

"What about us?" she asked.

"I miss you."

She didn't speak.

He continued.

"I miss the way you used to hum when folding laundry. I miss the way
you always added cinnamon to the coffee, even though you pretended you
didn't."

Her eyes closed for a moment.

She remembered the way he touched her shoulder

when passing behind her in the hallway.

The smell of his skin after mowing the lawn.

The feel of his breath on her neck in the deep of night—

long before the silence between them became a chasm.

"I still do," she said.

"Still do what?"

"Add the cinnamon."

A long pause.

Something unspoken bloomed between them—

not joy.

Not grief.

Something different.

"You don't have to say it," he whispered.

"What?"

"That you still love me."

She didn't answer.

Didn't need to.

The silence answered for her.

"It means everything, Miriam," he said.

"That you're still here."

"I'm not going anywhere," she said.

"Where would I go?"

Another pause.

And then, his voice changed.

Not in pitch.

But in weight.

He cleared his throat again.

"There's something I need to tell you. Before someone else does."

She straightened in her chair.

The room stilled.

"What is it?"

"It's about Lauren."

The name pierced the room like a bell rung at the wrong hour.

She blinked slowly.

"What about Lauren?"

"I just—" he exhaled. "I want you to hear it from me."

A pause.

Then—

"The detective. Riddick. He's going to call you. Or maybe come by."

"For what?"

Another long silence.

Miriam could hear his breathing now.

Shallow.

Measured.

"Harlan?"

"I need to tell you what happened," he said.

"To her."

She sat very still.

The roast was burning.

Smoke curled faintly from the edges of the oven.

But she didn't move.

"She always had an attitude, Miriam. You know that," he began.

His voice was fragile now.

A thread pulled too tight.

"We were arguing at the top of the stairs."

He stopped.

Tried again.

"She came down the stairs fast. I meant to stop her. Just to stop her."

A sound escaped his throat.

Not a sob.

Not a growl.

Something between confession and collapse.

"She fell," he whispered.

"I hit her. She fell. Her head—"

Miriam closed her eyes.

But the tears didn't come.

"After," he said,

"I carried her into the garage."

No sound in the kitchen now.

Not even the ticking of the clock.

"I cleaned her," he said.

"Washed her hair. Her hands."

He inhaled.

"I used rosemary oil. I thought it might help. I thought—"

His voice broke.

"I wrapped her in her blanket. The purple one. The one she loved."

He was crying now.

Quietly.

"You don't understand, Miriam," he said.

"I loved her. I did."

She stood then.

Walked to the oven.

Turned it off.

The air was thick with burnt meat and rising smoke.

She didn't open the door.

She pressed her hand to the glass.

And stared.

When she spoke, her voice was quiet.

"You told me she ran away."

"I know."

"For years."

"I know."

"I looked for her," she said.

"Every time we passed the old high school. Every time the phone rang."

"I know."

Silence stretched like thread between them.

Too thin to hold.

"Where?" she asked.

"What?"

"Where did you bury her?"

A long breath.

"In the yard."

"The old house?"

"Yes."

Miriam's fingers curled around the cord.

White-knuckled.

The air shifted.

Something flickered at the corner of her vision.

A shimmer across the hallway glass.

"But we didn't move until a year later," she said.

"I know," he said too quickly.

She didn't speak.

Didn't breathe.

The line vibrated in her hand.

"I'm sorry, Miriam."

She said nothing more.

There was no more to say.

Only silence now.

A silence made of thirty years.

He whispered one last thing.

"I'm sorry."

The line did not disconnect.

But the words were done.

Miriam stood alone in the kitchen.

The air burned with rosemary and ash.

And on the other side of the mirror above the stove,

Temperance watched.

Not as wrath.

Not as mercy.

But as memory made flesh.

Bearing witness to the cost of silence.

CHAPTER 33:
THE TRACE

Florida – Winter 2021

The house had grown restless again.

Kathy hadn't slept in three nights.

The mirror above the mantle had started to mist—not from heat or weather, but from something behind the glass. The windows refused to stay closed. The floors creaked at strange hours, as though someone was pacing in a pattern they could no longer remember.

And then Temperance appeared.

Not as smoke.

Not as flicker.

She simply was.

Standing in the hallway like she'd stepped out of Kathy's breath.

Kathy didn't scream.

Didn't flinch.

They had known each other too long for fear.

Temperance said nothing.

Only moved—slowly—into the study.

Kathy followed.

The desk lamp flickered as they passed.

The laptop was open.

Temperance reached a hand—not to the keys, not to the screen, but above it, hovering.

She stared at the glow as though it were a mirror.

And then she turned her face toward Kathy.

Her eyes wide.

Insistent.

Kathy sat.

Typed without knowing why.

Rockweiller home, Hamilton Michigan, backyard.

Google Earth.

The satellite map took its time loading.

It felt... wrong, to look at it this way. Like trying to remember a funeral through a postcard.

But there it was—the long fence, the shed, the swing set.

She clicked closer.

Zoomed.

Panned.

Nothing.

Just grass. Trees. Shadows.

She dragged the view to the edge of the property.

Her hand froze.

There.

A clearing.

Subtle.

Wrong.

Too perfect to be natural.

A circle—faint, but visible—where the grass refused to grow.

Near it, stacked barrels.

She could only make out the outline of them.

Gray-blue. Lidded. Waiting.

Her throat closed.

She turned, but Temperance was gone.

Only the faint shimmer on the window remained, as though the glass itself had held its breath.

Kathy called Riddick the next morning.

He didn't answer.

She tried again.

Left a voicemail.

And then another.

Finally—he picked up.

"Kathy," he said, his voice half-patient, half-bracing, "you can't see evidence from Google Earth."

"You don't understand," she said. "Something is buried there."

"With respect, Ms. Badger, we've been over this. If you have more—"

"It's not a feeling," she snapped. "It's a fact. You need to look again."

A pause.

Silence heavy on the line.

Then: "We'll send a team. But if the cadaver dogs don't hit—"

"They will," she said.

But they didn't.

That afternoon, Riddick called back.

His voice was careful.

Flat.

"No scent detected. Dogs walked right past the barrels."

"Because he wrapped her in plastic," Kathy whispered.

Pause.

"We're closing the lead for now."

"You're making a mistake," she said.

He didn't answer.

Only hung up.

That night, she paced.

Each time she passed the mirror, she saw herself. Temperance.

She could keep still.

She knew and needed to act.

The computer screen glared.

She searched.

Airline tickets.

Michigan.

She arrived the next day at the police station.

Waited in the lobby, determined.

Refused to leave.

An officer offered her a coffee.

She declined.

Temperance stood by the vending machine, silent as a statue.

Hours passed.

Finally, Riddick came out.

"Ms. Badger—what the hell are you doing here? Don't you live in Florida!"

"Walk the yard yourself," she said.

"Look with your eyes. Not theirs."

He didn't respond.

Only nodded once.

That was all she needed.

* * *

Riddick stood at the edge of the Rockweiller property two days later.

The trees leaned in as if listening.

Frost rimmed the grass.

He walked the perimeter slowly.

Stopped by the shed.

The barrels were still there—silent, sun-bleached, untouched.

He squatted low.

Ran a gloved hand over the rim of the topmost barrel.

Something oily stained the lid.

Behind him, the woods creaked.

No wind.

No birds.

Just the sound of the earth holding its breath.

He turned.

Nothing.

But the hairs on his neck stayed raised.

CHAPTER 34

THE BARREL

Muskegon County Jail – February 2021

Detective Riddick returned alone.

No camera.

No partner.

Just the file under his arm, and the weight of a truth too old for procedure.

The door locked behind him.

Harlan didn't look up.

He sat hunched at the table—hands folded, body slack, as though something had already left him.

Riddick pulled out a chair.

Didn't sit.

Not yet.

He opened the folder.

Inside: a single photograph.

The barrels.

Half-buried in winter grass.

The faint shape of plastic blooming from the lid of the one closest to the tree line.

He slid it across the table.

"You lied."

Harlan blinked.

Once.

Slow.

"I edited," he said.

"To protect who?"

"To delay what."

Silence settled between them.

The kind that doesn't wait for permission.

Riddick leaned in, voice low.

"Is it her?"

Harlan nodded.

Barely.

Riddick exhaled once through his nose.

"You told your wife you buried her at the old house. That you gave her some kind of proper burial!"

"I needed her to forgive me."

"And now?"

Harlan looked up.

His eyes were hollow.

But not dead.

Haunted.

"Now I'm out of lies."

The air in the room changed.

Not temperature.

Not pressure.

Just... alignment.

Like the walls had shifted a fraction of an inch.

Like something was listening.

Riddick felt it too.

The tremor in his wrist.

The way the lights hummed louder.

He didn't speak.

Waited.

And Harlan broke.

Not loudly.

Not with confession.

With a gesture.

He reached for the paper cup on the table.

Tipped it.

Empty.

Still, he cradled it in both hands.

"When I moved her," he said, voice thin, "she was in the barrels –
inside the old garage."

He didn't flinch when he said it.

But Riddick did.

"The body?"

"The girl."

He paused.

Eyes unfocused.

"It didn't feel right, leaving her behind. That house didn't... deserve
her."

"And this one did?"

"It had roots."

Riddick swallowed.

Then—

a shift.

Not in the room.

In him.

His hand moved from the cup to his chest.

Pressed flat.

Right over the sternum.

"It came from here," he said.

His voice was different now.

Not theatrical.

But ancient.

"As if the ribs cracked open and the thing inside uncoiled."

Riddick stayed still.

Unblinking.

Harlan's fingers drew a slow circle over his chest.

"I didn't invite it."

He looked up.

"But I didn't close the door either."

A shadow passed behind his pupils.

Dark.

Glasslike.

And then—

a name.

Not whispered.

Spoken.

"Elara."

The light above them flickered.

Once.

Then again.

The temperature didn't drop, but Riddick's breath caught.

A pulse moved through the room—too slow to be wind, too fast to be real.

Something was coming.

Something was already here.

Harlan's eyes widened.

Fixed on a point over Riddick's shoulder.

He recoiled slightly.

Then smiled.

But it wasn't joy.

It was surrender.

"I told you," he said.

"It's not rage that drives it."

He closed his eyes.

"And it's not guilt."

Riddick turned.

Nothing there.

Only wall.

But the mirror on the far side of the room pulsed.

The silver blurred at the edges.

Then sharpened.

Temperance.

Standing just behind the glass.

Hands to the surface.

Face composed.

Terrible.

Sacred.

Watching.

"You see her," Riddick said slowly.

Harlan nodded.

Tears now.

Silent.

Steady.

"I always have."

His hands gripped the edge of the table.

Knuckles bloodless.

"She's not just a ghost," he said.

His voice cracked.

"She's the blood remembering."

Riddick stood.

Riddick gathered the photos.

Snapped the folder closed.

Paused.

"You'll be arraigned next week," he said.

"And after that, charged for her murder too."

Harlan didn't move.

Didn't blink.

Riddick turned to leave.

Harlan looked up.

"I want to tell you what it feels like."

A long silence.

Then, with a hollow voice:

"Like drowning."

A beat.

"And being the water."

Riddick opened the door.

The light flickered again.

A final stutter.

The door shut behind Riddick.

And the room exhaled.

As if a truth had finally been named.

And would not be buried again.

CHAPTER 35

THE DISCOVERY

Hamilton, Michigan – February 2021

It began with machines.

The dogs had found nothing.

Not the first time.

Not the second.

So they brought in the excavators—

a quiet fleet of steel and teeth—

and began to tear the yard open.

They did not say it aloud,

but the house knew.

The house had always known.

Miriam watched from the kitchen window.

She did not move.

Did not speak.

Just stood there,

hands resting on the edge of the sink,

watching the soil be unmade.

The earth folded back in layers.

Sod peeled like skin.

Topsoil lifted like old breath.

Each inch revealing what silence had hidden.

She stayed there for hours.

Even as the machines roared.

Even as the men with gloves and radios took turns marking
coordinates

and pressing long poles into the ground like dowels into memory.

She did not call anyone.

She did not cry.

She simply waited

for what she already feared was true.

They would find her.

And elsewhere—

not far,

but far enough—

Kathy sat alone in her car,

parked just outside the house where the excavating unfolded.

She had already seen it on the satellite images—

the place where the grass did not grow.

The barrels, half-visible in the filtered sun.

She had gone to the station.

She had demanded to be heard.

Now, she waited.

The phone on the passenger seat.

Her hands on the wheel.

The air too still.

The call came just after dusk.

A voice she had come to know—

Detective Riddick, steady and grave.

"We found something," he said.

And that was all it took.

Kathy stepped out of her car, a rental she had been using since arriving from Florida.

Without breath.

Without thought.

The air tasted of snow and broken things.

They began putting up a tent.

A gray dome over the place where the ground had been breached.

A surgical wound, open to the elements.

Lights hummed along its edges.

Officers moved like phantoms,

careful and quiet.

Kathy approached the edge of the site.

She did not flinch.

Temperance was already there.

Whole.

Still.

Her figure woven into the shape of shadow and breath.

She did not flicker.

She did not speak.

But the soil knew her.

And the air bowed around her like branches in wind.

Miriam remained inside.

She did not come out.

But she saw it all—

the officers in their muted choreography,

the shape of the barrel being lifted,

the bent tree beside the pit like a spine remembering pain.

She did not move.

Not until Kathy knelt beside the opening.

The barrel had split at the seam.

Plastic attempting to emerge.

Flesh peering through the film

as though it had been waiting for this moment.

Kathy reached into her coat.

Pulled free the small wooden cross she had carved weeks ago.

Pressed it into the soil beside the rim.

"This," she whispered,

"is where your name comes back."

Temperance stepped beside her.

Knelt without sound.

She placed a hand above the broken rim—

not touching,

but near.

And the wind stirred.

Not a voice.

Not a scream.

But a vow.

Detective Riddick knelt as well.

His voice gentler now.

"It was exactly where he said," he murmured.

"A barrel.

Wrapped.

Sealed."

He paused.

"There were… personal effects."

Kathy turned to him –

Calm, bright, unwavering.

"No. It is exactly where *I* said."

She looked into the earth.

And the earth looked back.

Behind the glass of the kitchen window,

Miriam's hand trembled.

Just once.

But she did not look away.

Riddick's voice caught.

"We'll confirm with DNA, but—"

"She was mine," Kathy said.

Not an opinion.

Not a hope.

A truth drawn in blood.

Temperance stood.

The snow began to fall.

Slow.

Soundless.

Like ash.

Like blessing.

And in that moment—

beneath the churning machines,

beneath the breach and the excavation,

beneath every lie that had settled over this ground like moss—

Temperance turned.

Her form shimmered—

not dissolving,

but returning.

She stepped into Kathy's shadow,

then deeper still.

Her outline faded—

bone to breath,

storm to pulse—

until there was no separation.

No flicker.

No veil.

Only Kathy.

Whole.
Restored.
The wind curled around her coat.
The soil softened beneath her knees.
And from the breach,
from the wound in the world they dared to name—

Elara rose.

Not in body.
In name.
In memory.
In knowing.
No longer buried.
No longer lost.

C H A P T E R   3 6 :
THE FUNERAL

Hamilton, Michigan – March 2021

The church was half full.

Not out of love.

Out of guilt.

Out of curiosity.

Out of the Midwest instinct to show up for tragedy wearing slacks and casserole.

Miriam sat near the pulpit, spine stiff, hands folded over her purse.

The program listed her as the mother.

The order of service included two hymns.

A reading from Psalms.

And three minutes of silence.

She had said nothing when it mattered. And now, nothing was what she carried. Silence wasn't just what she offered him. It was what she buried with Lauren.

Ok.Kathy sat near the back.

Black coat.

No tears.

She had not spoken during the service.

Had not looked at Miriam once.

But her silence was a roar—

a wave pressing against the walls of the sanctuary.

The pastor did his best.

Gentle words.

Vague blessings.

He said her name—Lauren—twice.

Kathy flinched each time.

There was no open casket.

No photographs.

Just an urn, silver and unremarkable, placed at the altar beside a wilting bouquet.

The remains had been cremated weeks ago,

when the full extent of the damage had become clear.

Neither mother could bear to see her like that.

No one should have to.

After the service, the people lingered.

They whispered.

Some hugged Miriam.

Few approached Kathy.

They sensed the fire in her.

They knew not to touch it.

The parking lot was half-melted snow and tire slush.

The sky hung low, thick with late-winter indecision.

Miriam approached with a small velvet bag in her hand.

Her shoes crunched on the gravel.

She held it out.

The second urn.

Smaller.

Lighter.

"I thought you should have part of her," she said softly.

"This is our daughter. Lauren belongs to both of us."
Kathy stared at the bag.
Did not reach for it.
Not at first.
Then—
with a sharp motion—
she took it.
Her fingers curled around the fabric like a hand closing over a wound.
"She's not Lauren," Kathy said.
Her voice did not rise.
It did not need to.
It struck like a hammer.
"Her name is Elara.
And I was the only mother she ever really had."
She turned.
Walked to her car.
Did not look back.
Temperance moved with her—
not beside, not behind—
but within.
Merged now.
Restored.
A flame no longer flickering.
Miriam stood in the parking lot,
hand still outstretched,
as if the gesture might undo what had just been said.
But it couldn't.
The funeral had ended.
The ashes had been divided.
The names had been spoken.
And the truth—
the terrible, sacred, blood-written truth—

had finally been heard.

Miriam turned back to the church.

Walked slowly to her car.

Alone.

Inside the velvet bag,

Elara's ashes rested against the heat of Kathy's palm.

Her name had returned.

Her story had survived.

And her mother—

her only mother—

would carry her forward now.

Not as memory.

But as fire.

EPILOGUE: THE CELL

The cell was small. Concrete walls, a narrow bed bolted to the floor, a stainless steel sink that never quite stopped dripping. The air was thick with the scent of bleach and old sweat.

Harlan sat on the edge of the bed, hands clasped loosely between his knees. His gaze was fixed on the floor, where a faint crack ran from the wall to the center of the room. He had traced it with his eyes countless times, memorizing its path, its tiny deviations.

There were no voices now. No whispers in the dark, no shadows moving just beyond the edge of vision. The silence was complete, oppressive.

He had told himself, for years, that it wasn't him. That the things he had done were the work of something else, something dark and separate. A demon, a presence, a force that had taken hold of him. It was easier that way. Easier to believe that he was a vessel, not the source.

But here, in the unyielding quiet, the truth settled in. There was no demon. There was only Harlan. Only the choices he had made, the lives he had taken, the pain he had caused.

He closed his eyes, but the darkness behind his lids offered no refuge. Images flashed—Elara's face, contorted in fear; the barrel, heavy and unyielding; the soil, damp and cold. Memories he could not escape, could not silence.

He had thought himself a monster, and in that, he was correct. But not because of some external evil. Because of himself. Because of the choices he had made, the paths he had taken.

The cell remained silent. No voices, no whispers. Only the drip of the sink, the crack in the floor, and the weight of his own thoughts.

And in that silence, Harlan sat, alone with the truth.

About the Author

Stone Eugene Clark crafts fiction shaped by psychological fracture, ancestral memory, and the quiet violence of belief—spanning literary horror, historical mystery, and the shadowed edges of crime.

Raised in the American West, he draws from buried archives, fractured faith, and ancestral memory to craft stories that bridge myth and blood.

For updates and contact:
Email: stoneeugeneclark@gmail.com
Instagram: @stoneeugeneclark

www.ingramcontent.com/pod-product-compliance
Lightning Source LLC
Chambersburg PA
CBHW032251310726

48973CB00008B/2382

9798218698027